# more with you

## Kaylee Ryan

The following story contains sexual situations and strong language. It is intended for adult readers.

Cover Design: Sarah Hanson Okay Creations

Editing: Hot Tree Editing

Formatting: Integrity Formatting

# dedication

To the readers who gave
*Anywhere With You*
a chance and asked for more.


This is for you.

~ 1 ~

# Aiden

I rest my sweaty palms against my thighs, trying like hell not to let it show that I'm nervous. I look across the room and see my two best friends huddled close. Liam has a death grip on Allison's hand. I can't help but envy what they have; they bring out the best in one another. I have to admit, at first, I was skeptical, but now, anyone can see how much they love each other. I try to catch a glimpse of Hailey from the corner of my eye. She's sitting with me. She says it's so she can avoid the "love fest" that is Liam and Allison. I think, just for today, I'll pretend that she's really here for me. That she's my girl. *I wish!* As if she can read my mind, I feel Hailey place her hand over mine. She laces our fingers together and gives my hand a tight squeeze.

"You don't have to sit with me you know," I tell her as I nod my head towards Allison and Liam. Inside, I'm screaming at myself to shut the fuck up. I want her to stay right where she is.

Hailey smiles at me and I can feel my heart rate increase. "I'm good," she says leaning her shoulder against mine as she winks.

Hailey is my best friend, Liam's, little sister. I met her when she was a sophomore in high school. She is short compared to my six foot three, but I would say she is about five foot seven. Her long black hair hangs past her shoulders. She has a body that can bring a man to his knees, and her striking blue eyes hold me captive. Her eyes are also a reminder that she is my best friend's little sister. Liam

1

and Hailey share the same eyes. It's apparently a dominant trait in the MacCoy clan.

I've always found her attractive, but over the past year, my attraction to her has grown tenfold. I have fought it daily and continue to struggle with how much I want her. I know that I should just go for it with Liam dating my little sister and all; it's just awkward for me. I spent the first three years knowing her, treating her like my little sister. There was no attraction, and then one day, it's like I finally woke up from fantasyland and I realized Hailey is all that I want. I want her, but it would ruin my relationship with Liam and Allison if things went wrong between us. Hell, I would miss Hailey's friendship too. Over the past year, the four of us have become a tight knit group. Allison and Hailey are roommates, just like Liam and me. When Liam and Allison started dating, we all just kind of fell into a routine. This left Hailey and I to partner up in our adventures, which was both torture and bliss all at the same time.

I hear cheers erupt from the other side of the room and look up just in time to see Liam pull Allison into him, lifting her off the ground and spinning in circles. Liam shouts, "North Carolina, baby!" and I smile. The North Carolina Panthers have chosen him. I watch as my two best friends celebrate. Liam heads to the stage to accept his jersey while Allison stands on the side with tears running unchecked down her face. This has been an emotional year for her, most recently the diamond sparkling on her left hand. Liam proposed to her last night and I have never seen her happier.

I'm lost in thought when my agent, who Liam and I share, walks over and asks me how I'm doing. I smile at him and lean back, not letting on that my insides are shaking. My future is going to be determined today. I look over at Hailey and she's smiling watching Liam and Allison in their celebration. Her fingers are still laced with mine and I squeeze her hand, silently telling her that I'm glad she's here. She tilts her head to look at me and I lock my gaze with hers. I can't make myself look away, and it appears that neither can she. I hear my name announced followed by the North Carolina Panthers. *Holy fucking shit!* Liam and I are going to the same team. I'm up and out of my seat, bringing Hailey with me. I embrace her and my hold is so tight I'm afraid that I'm hurting her. I pull back and she's looking at me like I just cured world hunger. She licks her lips, and without thinking, I crash my lips to hers. This is only the second time I have tasted her, and this time is just as good, if not better than the first. The first time was New Year's Eve. We were all at our place and Hailey was sitting close to me on the couch. I meant it to be a friendly peck, just a quick sample of what it would be like if she was mine, but Hailey deepened the kiss, and I lacked the want and the will power to pull away. I did eventually pull back and tucked her into my side. I was sure that Liam was going to lecture me, but he was so wrapped up in Allison, he never did. Not that he needed to. I knew what he would say as I had just spent the last several months saying the same things to him about Allison.

Hailey and I have never talked about that night. The night that I discovered that she has the lips of an angel. I think about it all the time. Where I get the strength to not make her mine is beyond me. I can only assume that it comes from the fear of breaking up our group and losing three of the most important people in my life. So each day, I continue to hide the fact that I want her.

Reluctantly, I pull my lips from hers and drop a kiss onto her forehead. I release her from my hold and make my way to Liam and Allie and engulf them at the same time. "Panthers, man. We're going to the same fucking team." I release them and strut off toward the stage to do the same hat and jersey dance Liam just completed.

I'm smiling so big I feel like my face is going to crack. This moment is surreal and my smile gets bigger, if that's even possible, when I think that Hailey was the one next to me when I heard the news. *Life is good.*

As I exit the stage, everyone is waiting for me -; my parents, Mr. and Mrs. MacCoy, Liam, Allison, and Hailey. I stop to stand beside Hailey. We are so close that our shoulders are touching. I want nothing more than to hold her close to me again and taste her. Unfortunately, that's not going to happen. I was lucky to sneak in our little celebration while no one was looking, but that ship has sailed. I need to remember what's at stake. As if she can feel the tension rolling inside of me, Hailey steps closer and hugs me. The hug is over just as quickly as it began, but those few seconds helped calm me. Hailey's arms are then replaced by Allison's.

"You did it, Ace!" she says as I hug her tight.

"Hey, now get your paws off my fiancée," Liam chides me. I can hear the smile in his voice. He just wanted to call her his fiancée, yet again. Damn, Allison has turned him into a sappy bastard. Never in a million years would I have ever imagined my best friend turning into Mr. Romance. They say love changes you, and Liam is a prime example of that.

After Liam and I schedule meetings first thing next week to meet with our agent for contract negotiations, we all head out to celebrate. We end up at the local steak house, and surprisingly, Liam and I are asked for our autograph before we can even make it to our table. This happened in college with younger kids and girls who were throwing themselves at us. This is different. These are grown men who love the sport who are now asking. *This shit is real.*

We finally break free from the crowd and make our way to the table my parents had reserved for all of us. Everyone is already seated. Mom and Dad at one end and Mr. and Mrs. MacCoy at the other. Hailey is sitting next to Mrs. MacCoy with the only empty seat being between Hailey and my mom. This is just another example of how we have been paired off over the last year. At first, it never bothered me, but the closer Hailey and I become and the more I get to know her, the harder it is for me to resist her. The fact that she looks hot as fuck tonight, is so not helping.

Taking a deep breath, I slide into the seat next to her. This table is supposed to be a table for eight, but with four rather large guys, it's more suited for six. This means that my thigh is resting against hers. I know it's wrong, but I gradually scoot a little closer, just to be near her. No one at the table pays attention; they're all wrapped up in the menu discussing what they want. Hailey on the other hand, well, she notices. Her eyes find mine in question, so I wink at her. Yep, I decide to be my normal flirty self and act as though my entire body is not on fire for her. *Good plan, Emerson!*

Hailey, the minx that she is, winks back and licks her lips. *GAH!* She can't possibly know what that does to me, or she wouldn't keep doing it. On second thought, yes she would. Hailey and I have very similar personalities. We both flirt, harmlessly of course, and we both like to laugh and have a good time. Just another reason why I want her.

# ~ 2 ~

# Hailey

Today has been surreal. I was able to witness my brother and his best friend accomplish their dreams as they were both drafted into the NFL. The icing on the cake is that they were both picked up by the same team. I know their dynamics on the field had a lot to do with this as well as their agent. On the field, they are always in sync. This is why they were able to lead UNC to their third championship in a row this past season. They both deserve this and I cannot be happier for them.

As I sit here at the restaurant listening to the conversations and excitement, my mind drifts to earlier and the kiss between Aiden and I. For some reason, tonight I can't seem to get him out of my head. I'm pretty sure that it's not just the kiss. My hormones are in overdrive having to sit so close to him all night. If we were sitting any closer, I would be on his lap. Would I mind that? Hell to the no. Aiden on the other hand, probably would. He doesn't need me, his "friend," cramping his style. I've been in love with Aiden for what seems like forever. It started out as a crush on my brother's best friend. That crush has grown into love. Aiden is six foot three with shaggy brown hair. He has a lean yet muscular build, that of a runner. This of course works in his favor since he was just drafted as running back for NC Panthers. I have worked hard to hide my feelings for Aiden. I know a relationship would complicate things within our group. I also don't want to lose him in my life if things were to go wrong between us. I've done really well with hiding it except for my slip-up before I knew that Aiden was Allison's Ace. I told her how attracted I was to him, only to find out the next day that he is her best friend. They actually consider each other adopted siblings. At first, I wasn't sure how to take their relationship. They both said it was a sibling love they have for one another, and once I saw the connection Allison has with Liam, there was not a doubt in my mind that is all there is between the two of them. Anyway, after my little slip, I made an extra effort to be nonchalant about my feelings for Aiden. Allison has questioned me a few times and I avoid the conversation all together. Childish, yes, but I'm too afraid to let her know. What if he never feels the same? What if he does and then changes his mind? Too many risks. Either way, I think she's onto me.

Today was the second kiss that Aiden and I have shared, and just like the first, it left me wanting more. More than anything, I want to be that person for him. I want what Liam and Allison have, and I want it with Aiden. I know it's a pipe dream, but it's mine, and I'm holding it close to my heart for now.

"Hey, where are you?" Allison says as she links her arm through mine.

I break away from my thoughts and realize that she and I are the only ones left at the table. "I was just thinking of how happy I am for those two." I motion my head towards the door where the rest of our group is standing while my dad and Mr. Emerson argue over who is paying the bill. *Our families mesh so well together.*

"Me too." She is glowing with happiness. She has come a long way since her Gran died. We were all worried that we were not going to be able to pull her back to the old Allison. After our trip to Tennessee, she seemed to be coping better. Of course, a lot of that has to do with my brother and the way he dotes on her. I always told him that he was going to fall and fall hard, but damn that boy is weak when it comes to Allie. Liam is a big guy and can often be intimidating, but one look from my BFF brings him to his knees. He is constantly touching her; telling her how much he loves her. My brother is whipped. I smile because his whipped ass is making my BFF my sister, and I couldn't have picked a better person for either of them.

As Allison and I stand up to leave, she lets out a squeal. I turn to see that my brother has snaked his arms around her and has his face buried in her neck. Like I said, whipped.

Aiden appears. "Let's go, lovebirds," he says as he places his hand on the small of my back and leads the way to Liam's Pathfinder. He opens the front passenger door for me as he smiles and shakes his head. "No point in making them suffer," he says, laughing.

I nod my head in agreement, those two are inseparable.

"So, Hales, are you staying at our place tonight or do you want me to drop you off at the dorm?" Aiden asks as he pulls out of the parking lot.

Allison doesn't give me the opportunity to respond. "She's coming home with us, Ace. We have more celebrating to do," she chirps.

Aiden glances at me before focusing his attention back on the road. "You okay with that, Hales?"

My hand apparently has a mind of its own, because the next thing I know, my hand is on his thigh and I'm responding. "Yeah, sounds like a plan." I feel Aiden shift underneath my palm and I quickly move my arm back to rest on the console. I see his jaw tighten out of the corner of my eye. He then rests his right arm on the center console as well, and loosely twines our fingers together. There is no way that Liam and Allison could tell this is happening, even if they were paying attention to us. It seems as though since New Year's Eve, the lines have started to blur. We touch more, or maybe I just notice it more because his touch sets me on fire. Case and point, I can still feel the heat of his hand on the small of my back where he led me to the car.

Once we arrive at the condo, Allison and I head to the kitchen to gather the champagne and snacks that we hid earlier. Presumptuous of us, yes, but what can we say, we had faith in them.

"So, are we gonna talk about that kiss earlier?" Allison asks me.

"No, it was nothing. We were both caught up in the moment." I shrug my shoulders, acting as if it was no big deal.

"Um hmm," she winks at me.

"Charlotte is about a three hour drive with traffic. How do you think you and my brother are going to handle the distance?" I ask her, changing the subject.

"I don't know," she whispers while chewing on her bottom lip. "I can't stand the thought of being away from him. I mean, I know he'll have away games just like he did with UNC, but that was only for a few days at a time. Three hours is too far to drive each day with classes." She takes a deep breath. "We haven't had a chance to talk about it."

Liam and Aiden come strolling into the kitchen. Apparently, we're taking too long. Either that, or my brother is having Allison withdraws. "Haven't had a chance to talk about what, baby?" he asks her as he pulls her tight against him.

The look in Allison's eyes tells me that she's afraid of long distance. I can understand with losing her Gran recently. We're all she has, and I know being all alone is her fear. She is still chewing on her lip and my heart aches for her with everything that she has gone through.

"Allie and I were just talking about how long it takes to get to Charlotte from here. I asked her how you all were going to handle the distance," I tell my brother. He is shaking his head no before I even finish.

"No distance! Allison is coming to Charlotte with me." He turns her to face him, cupping her cheeks. "Right, baby, you're coming with me to Charlotte? I can't be that far away from you every damn day." He kisses her forehead. "Not gonna happen, beautiful girl."

I look away from the love fest and see Aiden watching me. He smiles a shy smile, almost apologizing for getting caught. "All right you two, I thought we were going to celebrate. You can do that on your own time. Hales and I don't want to lose our dinner." He winks at me.

We all laugh as we make our way to the living room. The rest of the night is more laughing and joking, We Talk about the NFL and their move to Charlotte. I can't help the ping of sadness I feel that my group is leaving me. The three of them are moving to Charlotte and I'm going to be here in Chapel Hill…all alone.

I shake the thoughts away and rejoin the conversation. Allison is watching me closely, being my best friend, she knows when something is bothering me. I smile at her to let her know I'm okay.

"Well, training camp is only, what, six weeks away? I think we need to plan a trip before then. Once camp starts you two are going to be busy for the next several months," Allison suggests. We can also celebrate Hailey's birthday while were there." She winks at me.

"Don't forget you have a wedding to plan, beautiful," Liam tells her as he pulls her on his lap.

Aiden and I both laugh out loud. It's still hard to see this version of my brother.

"How about the beach house? Mom and dad are never there. Even if they are, the place is huge. You two," I point to Liam and Aiden, "need to kick back and relax. Being rookies, you know they're gonna be tough as hell on you," I tell them.

"I'm in," Aiden says

"Sounds good, let's plan on leaving in two weeks. That should give us enough time to get our contracts squared away. Worst-case scenario, we have to come back for a day or two," Liam says.

After working out the details, Liam and Allison say goodnight and venture to their room. This leaves Aiden and me alone in the living room. "Feel like watching a movie?" he asks me.

"Yeah, I'm still on an adrenaline high. I can't believe my big brother is now a part of the NFL." I smile at him.

"Hey, what about me?" he pouts, sticking out his bottom lip and looking adorable. Truth be told, my adrenaline rush is just as much from our kiss as it is happiness for my big brother.

"Aww, did I hurt your feelings?" I laugh as I chuck a pillow at him and stand up. "I'll make some popcorn while you start the movie," I say over my shoulder as I walk away.

In the kitchen, I rest my elbows on the island and place my hands on my temples. I have to get a grip on my emotions. I can't let Aiden see how he's affecting me. Hiding how I really feel about him is harder when it's just the two of us. There's no one around to

9

buffer and distract me. Once I feel a little more composed, I pop two bags of popcorn and place them in one large bowl. I grab us both a water out of the fridge and make my way back to the living room, back to Aiden.

He's sitting on the loveseat, wearing gym shorts and a t-shirt, and holy hell, he is HOT! As I walk closer, his eyes meet mine and he graces me with one of his sexy grins. He pats the space next to him. "I saved you a seat." He reaches for the waters and sets them on the end table. He then takes the bowl of popcorn out of my hands and does the same thing.

I sit down beside him and curl my legs underneath me. Aiden pulls my favorite chenille throw from the back of the loveseat and places it over my legs. He then slides himself under as well, covering his lap. Without saying a word, he reaches for the bowl of popcorn and places it between us, resting half on his lap and half on mine.

Needing to focus on something other than the warmth of him next to me, I ask, "So what are we watching?"

"Remember, you said I could pick the movie. So…I went with a horror flick." He smirks.

"So, when I wake you up from my nightmares, you'll have no one to blame but yourself," I chide him. I no longer care what the name of the movie is; I'll spend at least seventy-five percent of it with my head buried in a pillow. *Asshole!* At least my mind will be on other things, even if it's fear.

Aiden rests his head on my shoulder. "I'll sleep on the couch so you're not out here alone, or better yet, you can just sleep with me." He lifts his head and shrugs as if the thought of us in bed together is nothing to him. Well, that's because it's not. He would shit if he knew the thoughts that I have been having about him.

"Just start the damn movie," I pout. At least I hope that's what I'm doing. I'm still trying to recover from the "you can just sleep with me" comment. What I really want to say is "To hell with the movie, take me to bed." Yes, my mind went there.

# ~ 3 ~

# *Aiden*

What the fuck am I doing? I can't believe that I basically just asked Hailey to sleep with me. Well, not really, but if she was in my bed, I don't think that I could not touch her. There have been several nights over the past year that I chose to sleep on the couch instead of my room, just to be next to her. I know she hates scary movies, and although it may sound cruel, I want her to need to be next to me tonight. Today was the biggest day of my life; the beginning of my future, and to end it with Hales curled up beside me, nothing can top this.

I drape my arm across her shoulder and tug her closer. "I'll protect you, sweetheart." Trying not to think about how great she feels in my arms, I grab the remote, hit play, and begin to stuff my face with popcorn.

Not fifteen minutes into the movie, Hailey has the blanket pulled up over her eyes. I place the popcorn bowl on the end table and finish off my water. I offer Hailey hers and she declines. "I'm good," is her reply. I don't think she even knows what I am offering her since her eyes are still closed and buried underneath the blanket. As the music on the movie changes, she chances it once again and slowly uncovers her eyes. Just as she does, there's a loud bang that rings from the television. Hailey jumps onto my chest and buries her face. *Yes!* This was my intention. I get to hold her without her knowing that this, her in my arms, is the perfect end to my day.

I wrap my arms around her and gently stroke her back, soothing her. After several minutes, which is not nearly long enough, Hailey pulls away from me. "Sorry, you know I don't deal well with scary movies." She blushes. Damn, if that doesn't make me hard as a rock.

"I don't mind. I know you're just watching this for me." I pull her back to my chest and kiss the top of her head. "Thank you." I don't need to say anything else. Hailey releases a heavy sigh and curls up on my chest. After a few minutes, I can feel her breathing even out and I know she's falling asleep. I resume gently stroking her back, lulling her to sleep. Her falling asleep allows me to hold her longer. Why I torture myself, I don't know. I know what I'm doing is wrong, but I can't resist her.

The movie ends and Hales is sound asleep. I reach for the remote and pull up the DVR. Allison made sure she recorded the draft, so I decide to see what a schmuck I look like on television. I settle in with Hales tucked in close and watch as many others, just like Liam and I, were rewarded with a future that was once just a dream. Liam is up next and the camera pans to the embrace that he and Allison shared. I can't help but feel the pang of jealousy that hits me. Those two are solid, and I want that. I pull Hailey in a little tighter. I want that with her. I watch a few more minutes, and then I hear my name announced. I focus my attention back on the television. What I see is Hailey looking at me with that look, the one that makes me lose all train of thought and has the ability to bring me to my knees. They show me pulling her close and smashing our lips together. I smile remembering the kiss. *Oh shit!* Here I thought that I got off easy with Liam being distracted. There is no way I'm going to be able to avoid this now. I need to warn Hailey. I briefly debate deleting it from the DVR, but I don't want to rob Liam and Allison of seeing their shining moment on the big screen, well sixty inch flat screen anyway. Besides, they will air this again over the next couple of weeks.

Hailey stirs and I realize the sun will be up soon. Even though it kills me to do it, I gently lift her and carry her over to her "make shift" bedroom. I place her on the futon and drape a quilt over the top of her. I gently drop a kiss to her forehead. It gets harder and harder to go to my room alone when I know that she's out here. So, instead of going to my room to sleep in my large pillow top bed, I lie down on the couch and face Hailey. I watch her sleep and chastise myself for not being able to shake this want that I have for her. I tell myself that it's Liam. That he's why I fight this pull. In reality, it's all me. I'm scared to fucking death I'll lose her. Right now, I have the security of knowing that she'll always be in my life. We will always be close friends. I just need to keep reminding myself that there will never be more. Losing her is not an option!

I wake up the next morning to the smell of coffee. I feel like I'm being watched. I lift my head from the couch, and I see Allison sitting in the chair with a smile on her face. She's holding two cups of coffee. "Morning." She hands me the extra cup.

I slowly sit up and take the cup from her. "Thanks," I say as I take a sip. I realize she's still watching me. "What?"

She darts her gaze towards Hailey. "How long are you going to keep trying to hide the fact that you have feelings for her?"

*UGH!* Ash, that's my nickname for her, has always been able to read me like a book. We've been best friends since she was ten, and she's just like my little sister. "Of course I do; we're all friends. I would be a dick not to," I say, avoiding the true meaning of her question.

Their bedroom door opens and I hear Liam making his way towards the living room. "Keep pretending, but I'm onto you, Ace," she whispers.

Liam comes strolling in and makes a beeline for Allison. He takes her hand and pulls her out the chair. He then plops down and gently eases her on his lap, careful not to spill her coffee, which she offers him. He pulls her back against his chest and kisses her temple. "Morning, beautiful girl," he says; then takes a large gulp of the coffee they are now sharing. This has become a habit; one that I never thought I would see Liam take part in.

"Hey, man," Liam says to me. "You look like shit."

"Thanks, I'm so feeling the love right now," I retort.

Liam looks at the couch and spies the blanket and pillow I was using. "You sleep on the couch again?"

*Fuck!* "Yeah, Hales and I ate some popcorn and watched a movie. She fell asleep, but I stayed up to watch some television." I shrug. "Just couldn't get wound down from the rush of the day I guess." My eyes dart to Allison and she's looking at me with that all knowing smirk. Damn, Damn, Damn! I need to be more careful of how I act around her.

"Morning, sleepyhead," I hear Liam say, and I swing my head to see that Hailey is awake. She's still lying on the futon all curled up with her hair a mess and sleepy eyes. Fuck me, I love sleepy Hailey.

"Hey," she rasps in that sexy morning voice of hers.

I can't take it. I need to get away to clear my head. I gulp down the rest of my coffee and burn my tongue in the process. Small price to pay if you ask me; considering, I want nothing more than to pounce on Hailey at this exact moment. I stand and take my cup to the kitchen where I quickly rinse and place it in the dishwasher. I rush to my room and grab my gym bag. I stop briefly at the living room door and announce that I'm headed to the gym. I don't give any of them the chance to say they will join me. I simply dash out the door.

# ~ 4 ~

## Hailey

I wake up to the sound of voices and I lay still. I can tell I'm in my futon, but I don't remember how I got here. The last thing I remember is watching a movie and falling asleep in Aiden's arms. He must have carried me to bed. I snuggle further into the cocoon of my covers as I remember the warmth from his body. Memories of last night flash through my mind, and I realize that now is not the time to get worked up over Aiden while everyone is sitting in the same room. I open my eyes and see my brother with Allison on his lap and Aiden sitting on the couch. It's easy to see that he slept out here again. I try not to let my imagination run away with thoughts of why he does that. Liam notices I'm awake and says good morning.

Aiden turns his head and his gaze catches mine. For a brief moment, there is an unfamiliar look in his eyes. I can't describe it, and it's gone before I can try to decipher what it was or the meaning behind it. Aiden jumps up and within a few minutes, he is saying that he is headed to the gym without another word.

"What are you lovebirds doing today?" I ask my brother and Allison.

Allison turns to look at Liam and smiles, he nods his head and leans in for a kiss. "Absolutely nothing," Liam tells me. "I am going to spend the day enjoying my beautiful fiancée."

I roll my eyes at them, because really, can they be any more perfect. I love them both dearly, but this is my older brother and my best friend after all, I have to give them a hard time.

"Brown Chicken, Brown Cow," I say in my sleep ridden voice.

Allison's face goes beat red and Liam smiles smugly at me. "Do you blame me?" he says, never taking his eyes off Allison.

"Ugh! I need to head back to the dorm to shower. Are you all going to mom and dad's for dinner tonight?" I inquire.

Allison nods her head yes, as Liam is shaking his no. "Baby, we have to go. They look forward to this every week," Allison says. With that, my brother concedes like the whipped puppy that he is.

"Hales, we can swing by the dorm and pick you up." Liam tosses me his keys. "Take the Pathfinder and we'll have Aiden drive us."

Gripping the keys tight in my fist, I drag myself out of my nest and gather my things. Liam tells me to be ready to go at five, as I walk out the door.

The drive to the dorm is short, only ten minutes. I haul my tired ass inside and immediately head to the shower. I stand under the hot spray, letting the heat massage my muscles. Thoughts of last night invade my head. I can still feel Aiden's arms wrapped around me, gently stroking my back. At first, I only pretended to be asleep. I didn't want him to stop. Eventually, his gentle touch lulled me to sleep. I don't remember getting into bed, so I know Aiden had to have put me there. I wish I could remember how it felt for him to pick me up in his arms and place me in bed. Actually, it's a good thing I was asleep. I don't think I could have not attacked him in that situation. I stand under the spray until the water runs cold.

I apply lotion all over my body and debate on what I should wear. Aiden will be at my parents for dinner, and I want to look good for him. Yes, I know this is insane behavior. Aiden has seen me at my worst over the years. In the back of my mind, I want him to see what he's missing. Which in reality is messed up because he doesn't even know how much he affects me, how much I want him. The kicker is that he never will. I like how close we all are. With Allison and Liam's wedding in the works, there are sure to be more events that the four of us will be attending, and I don't want things to be uncomfortable if we didn't work out. It's better that I just love him from afar. This guarantees that I will always have him in my life. I'll take him anyway I can get him.

I pull my royal blue sundress off its hanger and slip it over my head. The color of the dress really brings out my blue eyes. I leave my hair down; it's getting long, reaching the middle of my back. I apply a little mascara and lip gloss, slip into my old navy flip flops and flop down on my bed. I have a paper to write and it is already one o'clock. Time is not on my side.

# ~ 5 ~

# *Aiden*

I hit the gym hard. I abuse the treadmill like an old country road, before moving on to weights. The entire time, Hailey consumes my thoughts, last night consumes my thoughts. What the fuck was I thinking?

I wasn't.

I shouldn't have held her. Fuck! I can still feel her in my arms. I can smell her on my shirt. With the realization, I reach up and rip my shirt over my head. Lifting isn't helping, so I move to the back corner of the gym and begin my assault on one of the punching bags. Blitzen appears out of nowhere and grabs a hold of the bag. I begin to unleash, throwing punch after punch until I'm completely drained. I let my hands drop to my sides as I rest my back against the wall and slide to the floor. Blitzen hands me a towel and a bottle of water before sliding down the wall to sit beside me. We sit in complete silence until I finish off my water.

"Who is she?" Blitzen asks with certainty.

"Humph!" I'm afraid if I say more, my dumb ass will spill my woes. The last thing I need is for him to know how much I want Hailey.

Blitzen chuckles. "Deny it all you want, man. Known you a while now, and I've never seen you beat the shit out of a bag like that."

I pull my legs to my chest and lean my head forward, letting it fall against my knees. I focus on taking deep, even breaths in and out. Blitzen sits patiently next to me. Blitzen aka Cole, Liam, and I have been close since freshman year. Blitzen is all about living life to the fullest and having fun. Very rarely does he open himself up to serious conversation. Can I trust him with this? Can I tell him that I want our best friend's little sister with an intensity that burns inside me? *Holy shit, I sound like Liam!*

With the realization that I'm starting to think like Liam, I know I'm in deep. *Fuck it!* I decide telling someone might help me work this shit out of my system. Allie is not an option, since she's best friends with Hales and attached to Liam's hip. I take a deep breath and lift my head, still avoiding Blitzen's gaze and staring straight ahead. I decide it's just like ripping off a band-aid. I spew it out before I lose my nerve. "I want Hailey. So fucking much."

I continue to stare at the wall in front of me until the sounds of the gym echo in my ears. Total silence from Blitzen. Curiosity getting the best of me, I turn my head to face him. He's smirking at me. I raise my eyebrow in question and he throws his head back and laughs.

"What the fuck, man?" Anger lacing my voice.

"Dude, this is not news to me." He slaps my shoulder. "Anyone with half a brain, or should I say, anyone who is not in their own little "love" bubble, can see how you and Hales feel about each other."

I whip my head around to face him, turning my body at the same time. "What did you just say?"

Blitzen grins like he just won the damn lottery. "You heard me. You and Hales have been dancing around each other for months." He shrugs. "Liam is too wrapped up in Allie to see it."

With that, I'm speechless. What can I possibly say? I can't deny it. Then his words sink in... *"You and Hales have been dancing around each other for months."* What?

"Did you..." I stumble over my words at just the thought that she could even remotely feel the same way about me.

20

"You heard me. Hales is into you. Maybe I can see it because I don't have anything vested. The four of you are tight." He shrugs.

Resting my head back against the wall, I close my eyes and let his words sink in. I briefly let my mind wander to last night and how it would have felt to hold her, knowing that she was mine. Jumping to my feet, Blitzen following suit, I stalk to the locker room to grab a shower. "It doesn't matter," I say, shaking my head. "I can't be with her. It would complicate things if it didn't work, and I can't chance her not being in my life. Not an option."

"Dude, Liam just proposed to your little sister," he reminds me.

Shaking my head, I explain, "Yes, but Hales and I are really good friends. I can't even think about her not being there. I would do something to fuck it up, and then where would we all be? It would be awkward and uncomfortable, and I would be without her." I grit my teeth at the thought. "Can't let that happen, my man." With that, I step into the shower.

Walking into the apartment, all is calm. I walk over to the couch and pick up my blanket and pillow from last night. I glance at the futon where only Hailey sleeps. I can still see her there curled up on her side, sleeping soundly. I must have watched her for at least an hour before I drifted off to sleep. Shaking my head to erase the thoughts, I make my way to my room. Just as I stop to open the door, Liam's bedroom door opens. "Hey, I didn't think you guys were here," I tell him.

Liam lifts his fingers to his lips as to tell me to be quiet. "Allie is sleeping. We're just hanging out here today."

"Where's the Pathfinder?" I question.

"Hales took it. We need to stop and pick her up on the way to mom and dads."

"What time are we leaving?"

"I told Hales we would be there at five."

"Sounds good, man. I'm going to take a nap. Didn't sleep the greatest last night." *Shit!* Why did I bring it up? *Shit, Shit, Shit!*

"What's up with you sleeping on the couch anyway?"

Liam has asked me this question many times, and I've always been able to dodge him. This time, I don't think I'm going to be that lucky. Once he watches the draft, he's going to know that I sleep on the couch for more than just the simple purpose of falling asleep there.

"Hales and I were watching a movie. She fell asleep, but I stayed up to watch the draft." It's out there. Now all I have to do is wait for Liam to watch the draft and kick my ass. *Fun times!*

Liam eyes me in question, but doesn't comment further. "I'll be ready to go by five," I say as I push through my bedroom door, closing it behind me, and plopping down on my bed. I can hear Liam make his way to the living room. My guess is that he's going to watch the draft. I need to get my shit together before he questions me. I know it's coming.

As I'm lying in bed, I can't turn my mind off. I know my best friend is getting ready to watch, if he hasn't already watched, me attack his little sister with a scorching kiss that would have brought me to my knees if it were not for the excitement of being drafted. I toss and turn, unable to get comfortable. Finally, I decide to face the music. I figure it's easier to face Liam alone than with Allison by his side. She has always been able to see right through me. She already has her suspicions about Hales and me.

I stop by the kitchen and grab a bottle of water before joining Liam on the couch, just in time to watch the last few minutes of the recording. Liam reaches for the remote and turns off the television. *Here it comes.*

"So, not that I have any room to say anything…but what the fuck was that with my sister?" he asks with controlled anger. I'm actually surprised he's being as calm as he is. Although, I know he would hate to wake Allison with his anger. She would be all up in his shit.

Taking a deep breath, I try to explain, "It was the moment, man. Hales and I are really good friends. I had just finished watching you and Ash celebrate, and I just wanted that. I wanted to share it with someone." I take another deep breath. "I got carried away. It won't happen again," I say with sincerity, even though I'm torn. I want nothing more than to do exactly that, kiss her senseless over and over again.

"Looked like a hell of a lot more than just getting caught up in the moment," he snarls at me.

So far, so good. I can tell he's pissed, but he hasn't thrown any punches yet. Maybe I can be a little honest with him and see how he takes it. "Yeah, man, it was. I mean, Hales is beautiful." I run my hands through my hair. "It's hard not to be affected by that, you know?"

"Fuck!" Liam stands up and paces in front of the television. "What am I supposed to say to that? Are you interested in Hales? My baby sister? What the fuck, man?"

I can feel my heart starting to race. "Really, dude? You're gonna pull the fucking baby sister card on me? Really?" I stand and walk towards him, standing toe to toe. "Did you already forget that you are engaged to *my* baby sister? Did you already forget who lays in your arms at night?" I take a deep breath. Taking it in slowly and releasing. I'm pissed because I want Hailey, and she will never be mine! I'm pissed because Allison is my baby sister, and Liam is quick to forget that.

Liam raises his finger and places it on my chest. Just as he is about to lay into me, I hear Allison.

'What the hell is wrong with you two?" she rants as she stomps into the living room. I see her eyes widen, taking in the scene before her. "What's going on?"

Liam immediately drops his hand and walks towards Allison. He pulls her into his arms and kisses the top of her head. "I'm sorry we woke you, beautiful girl."

Allison pulls out of his arms and places her hands on her hips. "One of you better start talking," she demands.

Liam is not impressed with Allison pulling away; he reaches for her and she steps back. "You better start talking, MacCoy," she tells him.

Liam lets out a frustrated sigh. "I was watching the draft and saw Aiden kiss Hales," he whines.

"Okay, and…?" She looks between the two of us. "You were in his face because of a kiss? Your best friend? You looked like you were ready to thrown down."

I continue to remain silent. I make a mental note to give Allison the mother of all hugs once this is over.

"Well, yeah…I mean no. Fuck, I don't know okay. All I know is that he pulled her into a kiss that was more than just a friendly peck. He's my best friend and she's my little sister," Liam tried to reason. I can tell that even he is beginning to understand that what he is saying is hypocritical considering his relationship with Allison.

Allison walks towards me and wraps her arm around my waist, leaning into me, giving me a hug. "Yes, Hailey is your little sister." She looks up at me. "And, I'm Aiden's little sister." She doesn't say anything else and I can see that Liam is ready to accept defeat.

Liam stalks towards us and I brace myself for his wrath, but instead, he gently tugs Allison's arm and pulls her into his embrace. He crushes her to his chest and kisses the top of her head. "I'm sorry," he tells her.

"You don't need to apologize to me. Ace is the one you need to say you're sorry to." She rests her hand against his cheek. "There is nothing going on with them, and even if there were, wouldn't you rather her be with your best friend? Someone you trust with your life, rather than someone like Jason or Todd?"

Liam shudders at the thought; so do I. No way will they ever lay their hands on her again. *Over my dead body!*

Liam tucks Allison back into his side. "Dude, I'm sorry I went a little crazy." Allison rests her hand on his chest. He lifts it to his lips and brushes a kiss across her palm, before placing her hand back against his heart. "If you are interested in Hales, I don't have a leg to stand on. Just know that if you hurt her, I will fuck you up."

"I would expect nothing less," I tell him. "There really is nothing going on between us. I was caught up in the moment, and Hales is one of my best friends." I shrug my shoulders, hoping like hell that I appear as unaffected by the kiss as I'm trying to sound.

"Fair enough," Liam says. "We need to leave in an hour. Let's go take a shower, baby."

With that, the conversation is over and I'm in the clear for now. All except for the tightness in my chest from knowing that I just lied to two of the most important people in my life.

# ~ 6 ~

# Hailey

I am so engrossed in my paper that I am startled when Allison comes barreling through the door of our room. Actually, it's more like my room. She hasn't slept here in months, and most of her things have migrated their way to Liam's.

"Hey, how's the writing coming?" she asks cheerfully.

"Good actually. I'm just about finished."

"Good thing, the guys are down stairs ready to go."

I quickly save the paper and close my laptop. I grab my keys and wristlet, and follow Allison out the door, pulling it closed and making sure that it's locked.

"I don't really have a lot of time to explain, so the details will have to come later." She places a hand on my arm to stop me from moving forward. "Liam watched the draft today, and he saw the kiss between you and Aiden. He was pissed at first, but I gently reminded him that he is currently engaged to Aiden's little sister," she says this as she wiggles her ring finger in front of my face, flashing her engagement ring.

My palms are starting to sweat. Liam cannot find out how I feel about Aiden. *Shit, Shit, Shit!*

"It was nothing. We were both just caught up in the moment." *Liar!*

Allison starts walking again. "That's what Aiden said, so Liam has calmed down. I just thought you should know in case it gets brought up."

My heart drops at hearing that the kiss was just that, a kiss between two friends who were caught up in celebration. At least in Aiden's eyes. I swallow back the emotions threatening to spill over.

Allison pushes open the door to our building, and front and center are Liam and Aiden both leaning against the front of Liam's Pathfinder. "Let's get a move on, boys," I say in what I hope is a cheerful, not affected by Aiden, voice. I have to learn to be me, and want him from afar without anyone knowing. Maybe the distance in the fall will help.

Liam walks to the passenger side, opening both doors, one for me and one for Allie. Aiden slides in the backseat next to me from the other side. "Hey, you," he says playfully, nudging my leg with his.

"Hey, how was the gym?"

Aiden shrugs. "Same old, same old. I got it in."

"Allie, did you tell Hales that you found a few dresses online," Liam asks her.

"Oh my gosh! Hailey, you have got to see them. They are so gorgeous," she gushes.

"So when is this shindig taking place?" Aiden asks.

Allison laughs. "We haven't set a date just yet, but we will soon," she says while leaning over the console to place a kiss on Liam's cheek.

The remainder of the drive to my parents' is consumed with wedding talk. Liam wants to marry Allison tonight, but she is having no part of it. She talks about a small, intimate wedding with close friends and family. I hear the hitch in her voice at this point in the conversation. It's hard for her, not having any family. My heart breaks for her. I am so glad she came into our lives. She's one of the strongest, most loving people I have ever met. *She's going to be my sister!*

Walking into my parents' house, it's unusual that they are not at the door to greet us. "Mom? Dad?" I yell through the house, while the others trail behind me.

"Out here, Hales," my dad calls from the back patio.

Pushing the screen door open, I stop in shock. Sitting with my parents are Aiden's parents. They have met several times, but never 'hung out'.

Aiden makes his way to his mother and bends to kiss her cheek, before reaching out to give his father a man hug. "What's going on? What are you guys doing here?" he asks them.

"The MacCoy's invited us to dinner, and thought that Sunday would be a great time, since all of our kids would be here as well." Aiden's face is lit up with a smile and Allison has tears in her eyes. I can only assume it's from them referring to her as their kid. She embraces Mrs. Emerson and gives Mr. Emerson a kiss on the cheek. He apparently isn't satisfied with that, because he pulls her into a tight hug.

My dad walks over and puts his arm around me. "Well, now that the gang's all here, I'll light the grill." He drops a kiss on my cheek and saunters off to the grill, beer in hand. *Have I mentioned that I have amazing parents?*

I join my mom, Allison, and Mrs. Emerson at the table, while the guys all head towards the grill. What is it with the male species and their grills anyway?

"Allison, have you and Liam thought about the wedding?" Mrs. Emerson asks.

Allison's face breaks out in a huge grin as a blush stains her cheeks. "We have talked a little bit. We know that we want something small and simple."

Mom leans in, eating up every word of the conversation. "Have you set a date?" she asks Allison.

"If Liam has anything to do with it, tomorrow." I chuckle, as does my mom.

"Well, he knows what he wants. Who can blame him?" my mom replies. "Allison, I would be happy to help with anything that you need; don't hesitate to ask."

Mrs. Emerson places her hand over Allie's on the table. "You know I love you like my own, and would love nothing more than to be there with you through all of this. Michael and I have always thought of you as our little girl," she says, tears in her eyes.

Allison is fighting back tears and before she can reply, as if he can sense her sorrow, Liam appears in front of her, dropping to his knees. "Baby, what's wrong?"

Allie's tears slowly fall as she laughs through them. Resting her forehead against his. "Nothing is wrong, I'm happy."

"MacCoy, you better not be making my sister cry," Aiden says as he joins us at the table, taking the seat next to mine.

Liam glares at Aiden as he lifts Allison from her chair, and sits down with her on his lap. "You know better," he sneers.

Aiden bumps his shoulder with mine and winks. This is a game we've played many times over the last several months. We both know that Liam would rather cut his arm off than do anything to hurt Allison, or upset her. We, however, get our kicks by trying to accuse him of it anyway. I know it sounds terrible, but don't knock it until you try it.

Conversations drift. Allison and I talk with mom and Mrs. Emerson about wedding plans. The guys talk about football; shocker, I know. I'm still sitting next to Aiden, and I'm trying hard to ignore him and how much I want him. However, his knee keeps bumping mine, our elbows are rubbing, and we have reached for the pepper at the same time, twice. Needless to say, I am relieved when dad suggest we play a game of football; guys against girls. Normally I would bow out, but the thought of tackling Aiden to the ground raises my spirits. Besides, my big brother is officially a member of the NFL; I need to learn to embrace the sport for more than just cheering on the sidelines.

Aiden and Liam rise from the table, both pulling their shirts over their heads. *Holy shit!* I have to touch my chin to make sure that the drool I feel pooling in my mouth isn't running over and causing me to look like I'm having some type of seizure. This him shirtless. Regardless of how often, it always has the same effect on me. Aiden has a true runner's body. Lean. Fit. Ripped.

*Game on!*

# ~ 7 ~

# *Aiden*

Sitting next to Hales was a bad idea. To make matters worse, I continue to torture myself by bumping my leg with her's and rubbing elbows. Yes, I'm well aware that I'm causing myself more grief, but I'll take Hales any way I can get her. Mr. MacCoy suggests that we play a friendly game of pigskin, and I'm up and out of my chair. This has been a regular thing with us over the past four years. The only difference is that my parents are here, and now, so is Allison. Liam and I both make quick work of removing our shirts; we are playing shirts versus skins. The thought of Hales in nothing but the skin she was born in flashes through my mind. Although I know I shouldn't, I chance a look at Hailey and she is starting at me. I can't describe the look in her eyes. She notices me watching her and quickly turns her attention to my mom. I shake my head, clearing my thoughts, while following Liam and our fathers to the backyard.

Playing shirts and skins, the teams are totally off balance. All four of us on the "skins" team played high school and college ball. There is also that little known organization called the NFL that Liam and I are now a part of. The "shirts" don't stand a chance. Liam comes sauntering over, grinning like a fool.

"What they hell are you smiling about?"

Liam shakes his head no. "Can't tell ya, man. You get pissy when I do," he replies, smirking.

33

I can only assume that this has something to do with Allison. I may regret this, but I'm hoping that it'll get my mind off Hailey. "Lay it on me," I tell him.

Liam wraps an arm around my shoulder and leans in to whisper in my ear. He's acting like he's about to divulge a secret that will change the world. "I get to tackle my girl. I'm shirtless, and Allie can't resist me when I'm shirtless. This was the best fucking idea ever!"

Shaking my head, I push him away. "Dude, I so did not need that visual." In reality, I'm getting used to it. Even I can admit that they're perfect for each other. I still need to give him shit, it's in my job description as best friend.

Mr. MacCoy yells across the yard, telling us it's time to line up. He declares ladies first. Hailey lines up across from me, imagine that. Suddenly, my earlier fantasy of Hales in just "skins," and Liam's little tidbit of knowledge regarding him and Allison, has my mind wondering to places it should not be going. Before I know what's happening, I'm falling backwards to the ground and Hailey is in position to land on top of me. Instinct has me taking the brunt of the fall, while I wrap my arms around her to protect her from injury.

"Oomph." I take a deep breath, pulling oxygen back into my lungs. Hailey is completely still on top of me. My heart is racing and my mind is running sexy scenarios faster than I can comprehend. I reach up and tuck a lose piece of hair behind her ear. "You okay, angel?" Hailey's eyes widen at my endearment. Instinctively, I tug her tighter against me. I've never held her like this. We've kissed twice, yes, I'm keeping count, and we have shared hugs on many occasions. What I haven't done, is hold her next to me so close that every inch of her is touching every inch of me. So close that it's difficult to tell where she ends and I begin.

Hailey locks her eyes on mine. "Hey," she whispers.

In this moment, I want nothing more than to fuse my lips with hers and kiss her until we are both breathless. I want to kiss her until she knows how much I want her. I'm thinking of throwing caution to the wind and doing just that, when I hear Liam.

"Come on, Hales, isn't it bad enough you just took down an NFL running back? Give the guy a break and let him up." At this everyone laughs.

Hailey's face goes crimson. "Sorry," she whispers as she quickly stands and heads back to the line to stand beside Allison.

I'm lying flat on my back, staring at the blue sky. I shiver at the loss of warmth from having Hales tight against me.

*Fuck!*

Liam appears over me, shielding the sun. "You all right, man?"

"Yeah, I'm good. Just catching my breath. Hales knocked the wind out of me." I'm not exactly lying.

He reaches his hand out to help me up. Once I'm on my feet, I glance at Hales and she has her head back laughing at something that the other three are saying.

Beautiful angel.

"Come on you two, let's get this show on the road." This coming from my dad.

We line back up, this time I make sure that I'm across from my mom. Dad gives me a curious look, but I act as though I don't even notice. After all of the small touches at dinner and our recent tumble and embrace, I can't take much more. Hailey MacCoy is going to be the death of me.

We run play after play, and time seems to fly by. I make sure that I'm never lined up with Hailey. At one point, I look in her eyes…she looks upset. I want to pull her into my arms and explain that she's testing my will power. That I want nothing more than to be the one rolling around on the ground with her, but I can't. Losing her as a part of my life is a risk that I'm not willing to take. Losing her would break me.

# ~ 8 ~

## Hailey

What. The. Hell. Was. That.

Trying to get my bearings, I make my way back to my team, "the shirts". My mind is reeling with my encounter with Aiden. The way he was looking at me. The tenderness in his eyes, in his voice. *Holy shit!* My panties are wet from three little words. Aiden has never called me angel before. It's usually Hales and sweetheart, but that's a southern gentleman thing. Angel, yeah that's not.

I reach my team and catch the tail end of Allison explaining our "game plan". Apparently, we are handing the ball off to her and she's going to shake her ass at Liam to distract him. We all know there is no way he's going to give anyone else the opportunity to tackle her. I throw my head back and join them in laughter. Allison, my best friend, I can always count on her, even when she doesn't realize that I need her. Our moms head towards the line, which is also the middle of the backyard. Allison bumps my shoulder with hers.

"You okay?" I can see the question in her eyes. She has tried multiple times to talk to me about Aiden. I made the mistake a long time ago of letting her know that I have lusted after him for years. At the time, I had no idea that they were practically family, or that she would eventually marry into mine. I continue to tell her that there is nothing there, but Allie is perceptive. I need to step up my game if I plan to continue to hide my feelings for him.

Throughout the rest of the game, Aiden makes it a point to avoid me. I fight back the tears that are battling to push to the surface. I know deep down that Aiden doesn't want me, but until this moment, I've pretended that he did. That he wanted me and that maybe, just maybe, at some point in the future, we would both confess our love and live happily ever after. *Yeah right!* Aiden Emerson delivered me a gigantic dose of reality. He has no desire to be, and will never be mine. His actions confuse the hell out of me. He was so sweet and tender. He called me angel. Yet, he is going out of his way to avoid me. His temporary lapse in judgment must have worked into to the conscious part of his brain, telling him he needs to stay clear. *Mission accomplished, Emerson.* Mission Accomplished.

I feel a strong arm wrap around my shoulders. A scent that is forever ingrained in my brain, surrounds me. Daddy.

"Hey, baby girl. You ready for some dinner?" He kisses the top of my head.

I wrap both arms around his waist and hug him tight. "Yeah, let's go." We turn to walk back towards the house; my arms still wrapped around his waist. Dad stops his strides about halfway there, halting my steps in the process.

"You okay, Hales?" he asks, concern lacing his voice.

"I'm good, dad. Just a lot of emotions over the past several weeks; I think it's all catching up with me." I hear laughter coming from the porch I look up and see Aiden and Liam spraying each other with the water hose. My chest tightens at the sight of Aiden. I need time to clear my head, but the four of us are always together.

Dad follows my gaze and hugs me close. "Why don't you stay here tonight? I can drive you back tomorrow. Give you a break," he suggests.

"You know what? That sounds like a great idea. I would love to spend more time with you and mom."

"Come on, let's get some dinner" he says, tugging me along with him.

We make it to the patio and everyone is already digging into the leftovers. "What took you two so long?" mom asks us.

"I was just convincing my baby girl to spend the night with us. Give us all some time to catch up," Dad says.

I walk over and sit down beside mom; Mrs. Emerson is on the other side of her. I can't sit by Aiden. I have tortured myself enough for one day. Mom smiles at me, she's happy that I'm staying and that smile alone lifts some of the sadness in my heart. My parents are amazing people, and I hope to one day have a relationship like theirs.

The leftovers are just as good as they were the first time. Everyone thanks mom and dad, and Mr. and Mrs. Emerson decide it's time to head home. They have about a two -hour drive ahead of them. We all walk them outside and say out goodbyes.

"Well, we better head out too," Liam says. "You still staying here, Hales?"

Allison offers me a small smile. I chance a glance at Aiden and he's watching me, the expression on his face is blank. Unreadable.

Pulling my gaze back to Liam and Allison, I answer, "Yeah, I want to hang with mom and dad tonight. Dad said he would drive me back tomorrow sometime. I need to start packing up the dorm, so I'll get him to stop and get me some boxes on the way there."

"That's a good idea. Have him pick up a few extra so we can get the rest of Allie's stuff to our place," Liam says.

"Will do, big brother. You guys be safe," I say, giving Liam and Allison a hug goodbye. After releasing them, they head towards the car. When I turn around, Aiden is standing right behind me. I almost knock him over; he is standing so close. He tucks a lose tendril of hair behind my ear. "You okay, angel?" he asks me.

No, I want you. "Yeah, I'm good," I say, taking a step back. "I just want to spend some time with mom and dad. I'll see you guys tomorrow I'm sure."

Aiden doesn't say anything else. He nods his head in acceptance, steps in and gives me a tight hug, and then turns and walks away. My knees are shaking and my heart is racing. Definitely need a break.

I collapse on the front porch step and watch them drive away. Tears burn the back of my eyes. I'm going to miss the three of them so much. In just a few months, we will be three hours away from each other. Not too bad as far as distance goes, but I need to get used to it. Staying here tonight is a good start. Although I hate to admit it, I think distance might be my only hope of getting over Aiden.

I hear the front door open, and footsteps cross the creaky boards of the porch. Mom sits down beside me. I rest my head on her shoulder. We sit in silence for several minutes. She reaches over and lays her hand on top of mine. "Want to talk about it?" she asks quietly.

It's with those words that the dam breaks. Hot tears flow from my eyes as I silently cry over what I want, and what I know I'll never have. Mom wraps her arms around me, her way of telling me that she will always be there and everything will be okay.

"You know, Aiden feels the same way about you," she softly whispers.

I lift my head so I can see her face. "What? How?" I ask because, well, I don't believe that he does, and how the hell does she know everything?

Mom chuckles softly. "Hales, you have had your eyes set on Aiden from the day Liam brought him home for the first time. He looks at you the same way." She shrugs.

"Mom, he doesn't want me. You saw how he acted today. He went out of his way to avoid me all together."

"Yes, he did. He also looked at you like you were the air that he breathes. You were too wrapped up in avoiding him as well, to see the looks that he was giving you. You were looking at him the same way. Give him some time, sweetie. Aiden has not had these feelings as long as you have. If it's meant to be, it will happen. Jennifer and I both think you all will find your way together."

"What? You and Mrs. Emerson have talked about Aiden and me?" I asked, astonished at the thought.

This time, she full on laughs. "Yeah, we have. We see it in both of you. A mother knows these things."

I place my head back on her shoulder. "I needed distance," I tell her.

"Well, you know what they say? Absence makes the heart grow fonder. I saw the way he hugged you goodbye. He was not okay with leaving you here. Give it time; Rome wasn't built in a day."

I smile at her, "I love you, mom."

She gives me a hug that only a mother can give. "I love you too, Hales."

# ~ 9 ~

# *Aiden*

The drive back home is quiet. I'm driving while Liam and Allison are in the backseat, cuddled up together. *Bastard.* I hope he realizes how lucky he is. I drop them off at the dorms to get Liam's Pathfinder. I vaguely remember telling them goodbye. My mind is on Hailey. She looked so sad when I left her standing there in her parents' drive. I know I'm the reason she's sad, but fuck, I needed to stay away from her, or I might have embarrassed us both in front of our families. I hate that I'm the one who put that look in her eyes.

Before I even realize it, I'm pulling into the condo. I make my way inside and stop in my tracks. I see the futon that Hales always sleeps on, and she's not there. I want her there. I hear Liam and Allison at the door, so I quickly head to my room. I throw myself onto my pillow top mattress and wait for sleep to claim me. It doesn't. I reach for my phone, thinking that listening to some music will help clear my head and make me fall asleep. I open my music app and hit shuffle. "Rock N Roll" by Avril Lavigne begins to play and I smile. Hailey and Allison love this song. Allison insisted that I download it so she and Hailey could "rock out" a few weeks ago when we were all just hanging out. Instead of clearing my head, I think about how amazing she looked that night. They were both in flannel pajama pants and tank tops, not a stich of make-up, hair pulled up into a knot on the top of their heads. I slept on the couch that night too, just to be in the same room with her. Before I can stop myself, I'm opening the messages tab on my phone.

43

**Me:** Night, angel.

I wait with my phone clutched in my hand. Will she reply? Did I damage the relationship that I am so tightly holding onto? Before my mind can wander, my phone alerts me of a new message.

**Hailey:** Night.

I release the breath I didn't even realize I was holding. She responded, so that means she doesn't hate me. I need to keep my shit in check, so that my reaction this afternoon never happens again. Otherwise, I'll lose her anyway, without her ever really being mine. Yeah, that's not going to happen. Eventually I drifted off to sleep.

The next day, I wake up and find Liam and Allie in the kitchen making pancakes. I slowly shuffle my feet to the coffee pot and pour myself a cup.

"Hey, man, what you got going on today?" Liam asks me.

"Nothing, just hitting the gym. You?"

"Well, we are going over to the dorm to pack up the rest of Allie's things to bring them here. They have to be out of the dorms next week anyway. I was wondering if you might be able to help. I want to help Hales get all of her stuff too. I told her she could stay here. I think she's going to take over the condo when we leave."

"Yeah, let me get more caffeine in me and a quick shower, and then I'm all yours," I tell him.

"So your parents decided to let her live off campus? I'm going to miss her so much," Allison says to us.

"Yeah, apparently she's nervous about who she'll get stuck with as a roommate as most are staying together. Hales also sold the theory to mom and dad that we could all stay with her when we are in town to visit her." Liam chuckles. "Dad asked her how she knew we would be back, and of course, Hales's response was that 'she's too awesome for us not to'," he tells us, shaking his head.

Hell yes, she is. The thought of not seeing her every day is causing an ache in my chest. "She definitely knows how to work them," I say instead.

"Yeah, she always has," Liam says, while stuffing his mouth full of pancake.

Allison sets a heaping plate in front of me and my mouth waters. Having her here with us all the time definitely has its perks. I finish off my stack in record time, then hit the shower. As I'm dressing, my phone alerts me of a new message. I swipe my finger across the screen.

**Hailey:** Liam says you're helping today. Thank you

**Me:** Welcome.

What I really want to say is that I will always be there. I, however, need to keep it simple, keep my replies as if we are just friends. We will only ever be friends.

We arrive at the dorms around noon. Hailey and her parents have already made a pretty good dent. There are stacks of boxes in the hallway outside the door, so Liam and I begin carrying them down to his father's truck. Once all the boxes that were ready to go are loaded, we head back upstairs to help the girls pack.

There are six of us in their dorm room and boxes all over the place. It's tight quarters, and they have one of the bigger rooms. I see Hailey trying to lift a box off the floor. I reach her in time to place my hand on her arm to stop her. I bend down and pick up the box, she thanks me and I wink at her. That's what friendly, flirty Aiden would have done. "I got this, pixie," I chide her. She punches me in the arm with a smile on her face.

"I can take you, Emerson," she says, laughing.

Her laugh is music to my ears. I think Hales and I are gonna be okay. I just need to keep my game face on.

We spend the entire afternoon packing and loading boxes. "Well, I think that's the last of it," I say to Liam and his father.

"Thank God," Liam moans. "How did they pack so much shit in that little room?"

"Not going there, man." I know better than to let Allison or Hailey either one hear me talking about their "shit." I enjoy the meals they make us. I'm keeping my trap shut.

"Your mom and the girls are going to stay and clean, run the sweeper, scrub the bathroom. Why don't we head over to your place and unload?" his dad asks us.

"Sounds good, be right back," Liam yells over his shoulder.

"Where the hell are you going?" I yell back, knowing full well that he never leaves Allison without kissing her goodbye. *Damn, that boy is whipped.*

Ten minutes later, Liam emerges from the building and we are on our way to the condo. The drive is short, so we are there in no time. Mr. MacCoy backs his truck up to the garage so we can unload. I have never been so glad that our condo has an attached garage. Liam and I rarely use it. We have a weight bench out there that we moved to the corner to allow more room for the girls' stuff. Just as we are unloading the final box, the ladies pull up in Hailey's car. They climb out of the car, each one with their arms full. Mrs. MacCoy is carrying pizzas. Allison has a twelve pack of Bud Light and a twelve pack of Diet Coke, and Hailey has what appears to be chips, dip, napkins, and plates. *These girls are the shit!*

Mr. MacCoy runs to his wife's side and takes the pizzas from her arms. He then leans down and kisses her softly on the lips. She smiles up at him. Liam relieves Allison of her beer and Diet Coke and does the same. I take the bags that Hailey is carrying, but I don't lean down to kiss her. My lips ache to taste hers, to have one more sample of what she has to offer, but I stay strong, so instead, bump my shoulder with hers and give her a wink. "We better hurry inside in case it's contagious," I tell her.

Her eyes sparkle as she laughs and I again feel like all is right with the world. Hailey is happy, that makes me happy.

The next couple of weeks seem to fly by. Liam and I have meeting after meeting with our agent and the Panthers' reps. Contracts are discussed as well as the details of when to report to training camp. Liam and I also graduated from college last week, both receiving our Bachelor's degree in Sports Medicine. Our families once again got together to celebrate. This time it was at my parents' house. We were all worried how Allison would be, since her gran lived next door, but she handled it well. The house remains empty; she has yet to decide what she is going to do with it.

46

Allison and Hailey are living at the condo now full-time. I've offered Hailey to take over my room so she'll have more privacy, but she continues to decline. She says that she'll have the place all to herself soon enough. I don't know why it bothers me to have her out there when the rest of us are in private rooms. We rarely have the guys over anymore, it's just the four of us. I like it that way. I don't want things to change. I don't want to think about how things will be once we all move to Charlotte and leave Hales behind. Nope, not going there.

## ~ 10 ~

## *Hailey*

Living full-time with Liam, Aiden, and Allison has been a blast. The four of us get along well and we all usually ended up staying at their condo anyway. It's actually easier with not running back and forth to the dorm to get more clothes. Just a few more weeks until the three of them leave for Charlotte. The guys' agent is looking for a condo for them to share. They told him to look for a three bedroom so that I can have my own room when I come to visit. I try not to think about it. I'm just trying to enjoy each day as it comes. Once their lives with the NFL start, things are going to change.

Allison and I are currently packing for the beach house. We plan to spend at least two weeks there; which includes being there for my birthday. Aiden's parents and mine are going on a two -week cruise to Europe! I love how our families mingle so well together. I know my brother is thrilled, as is Allison, at this new friendship our parents seem to have.

"Make sure you pack that blue bikini we bought last week. It looks great with your eyes," Allison tells me.

"Oh, it's already packed and ready to go. I'm hoping it brings me luck with the fellas," I say with a wink.

Allison collapses on the bed in a fit of giggles and I follow her down. That's how Liam and Aiden find us a few minutes later. Apparently, our laugher led them to us.

"What's so funny, baby?" Liam asks Allison. He's watching her like she's a giant steak he wants to devour.

Allison looks at me and we lose ourselves in laughter once again. "I have to pee," she says jumping up and running to the bathroom, continuing to laugh hysterically.

Liam raises his eyebrow at me in question. I shrug my shoulders and try to compose myself. Allison returns a few minutes later, still smiling. She heads back towards the bed, but Liam cuts her off and pulls her into a hug. "Spill it, missy, or you'll be sorry," he tells her.

Allison bites her lip, trying not to laugh. "It was nothing. More of a 'you had to be there moment'," she tells him.

Unfortunately, that's not the answer he wanted to hear. He begins to tickle her, and she once again erupts with laughter, trying to fight him off.

"H-Ha-Hales, help me," she laughs.

I make my way to Liam, to attempt to help her in her efforts to be free. I plan to jump on his back and attack. Just as I'm about to pounce, I feel strong arms wrap around my waist from behind.

"Thanks, man," Liam says through his laughter.

I wiggle, trying to free myself from Aiden's iron grip, but it has the opposite effect. He tightens his hold on me. Leaning down, he whispers in my ear, "Don't fight me, angel, or you're next."

Hell with that! I continue to wiggle, and he pulls me so tight that I can feel him, all of him, against my back. I stop and remain still. Liam and Allison are in their own little world. This is risky to be this close to him like this. Feeling all of him. I again try not to think too much of it. He's a guy pressed up against a wiggling girl in short shorts and a tank top. What man wouldn't respond to that, right?

I feel his breath hot on my ear. Did he just growl? "Yes, angel, you did that. Now stay still so I can get myself under control before your brother kicks my ass," he roughly whispers.

I remain still like a statue. Aiden eases his hold on me, but doesn't let go.

I feel the thunderous beat of my heart, and Aiden. The heat of his body pressed against mine. It takes everything in me not to turn in his arms and press my lips to his. I want to wrap my arms around his neck and run my hands through his hair. I want every part of me forged with every part of him.

*I Want Him.*

I hear Allison squeal, and I'm brought out of my Aiden induced fog. I place my hands over his and pull them away from my hips. I step away from him before it's too late. Before Liam catches on and kills us both. I try to quell the excitement that I did that to him. For a brief moment in time, Aiden Emerson wanted me.

My chest is rising rapidly. I'm trying to pull oxygen back into my lungs. He makes me breathless. *He always has.* Although I know I shouldn't, I lift my head and chance a look at Aiden. He's staring right at me with a look that can only be described as lust. He continues to watch me, study me with those gorgeous brown eyes of his. I want to look away, but I can't force myself to do it. He looks as though he could devour me, and I don't want to miss a single fucking minute of it.

All too soon, our trance is broken when Allison frees herself from Liam, jumps off the bed, and runs to hide behind Aiden. He throws his head back and laughs at her. "Don't get me caught in the cross fire. You brought this all on yourself," he tells her, trying to step away to make room for Liam who is striding toward her with a wicked gleam in his eye.

He reaches around Aiden, grabs her arm, pulls her next to him, and kisses her senseless. My face heats with embarrassment. I turn my head and try to hide it. I've never been embarrassed by their many displays of affection. This time, it's different. This time, my awareness of Aiden and what just passed between us is still running through my mind. The thunderous beat of my heart and the ache deep in my gut is still pulsing with need. Need for Aiden, and to be in his arms. So yeah, I'm thinking of wrapping myself around him like a damn monkey, hence the embarrassment. Thank God, they can't read my mind!

Aiden places his hand on Liam's shoulder. "Dude, let her go. If they don't finish packing, we're never getting out of here. The beach is waiting for us." He laughs, and I'm sure it's because Liam just growled at him while still kissing Allison.

Needing the distraction, I grab ahold of Allison's hand and start pulling her away from my brother. "Chop, chop, missy! We have packing to do," I tell her.

Liam releases her, and we both quickly move to the other side of the room, laughing as we go. I am sure Allison thinks I am being a good friend and protecting her from Liam's lips. Nope, I need distance from Aiden. These next two weeks with just the four of us at the beach house is going to be a huge test of my will power. *Just friends, Hailey. You and Aiden are just friends.* I wonder how many times I will have to repeat it so that my heart gets the memo.

"You need any help, baby?" Liam asks Allison.

"No, now go away so we can finish." She pretends to be stern and upset; however, I can still see the hint of a smile.

"Awesome," Aiden says. "Let's finish packing up the truck; then all we will have left is to add their bags." He is already headed out of the bedroom door as he says it.

Looks as though I might not be the only one needing some distance. Doesn't really matter though, this day will be forever engrained in my memory. All of my moments with Aiden are.

~ || ~

# Aiden

I make the excuse of packing the truck and flee. Fleeing is really my best option. Option two was to haul Hailey over my shoulder like a fucking caveman and carry her to my room.

*Fuck!*

Now I have that image in my head.

Liam follows me outside. I wish he wouldn't. I just need a minute to calm the fuck down. I need time to compose myself; otherwise, I might end up blurting out how much I want her. Hailey, his little sister. I can still feel her tight little ass pressed against me. Yeah, this is so not helping me calm down.

"This is the last of it, other than the girls' bags. They each have two more, so they say." Liam rolls his eyes.

"Don't let Allie see you do that," I say, trying to get him worked up.

Liam wags his eyebrows at me. "I can make it better, trust me," he says with a smirk.

"Dude, my sister, remember?" I groan.

Liam just laughs and places the cooler in the back of his Pathfinder. I try to make it look like I'm searching for something in my bag to avoid making any more conversation. Right now, my mind is showing a Hailey reel, and Liam is not invited. I just want to savor the memory for a little bit longer. My wish is not granted as I hear the girls walking down the driveway.

"All set, beautiful girl?" Liam asks Allison.

"Yep, this is the last of it. Ace, you wanna sit up front with Liam?" she asks me.

Liam jumps in before I can even open my mouth. "Baby, I want you up front with me," he tells her, nuzzling her neck.

"Go ahead, Ash. I don't want to deal with his grumpy ass the entire way," I say, laughing.

She smiles at me, climbing into the front seat. I climb in the back and slide in next to Hailey. Liam being obsessed with having Allison as close as possible at all times is really starting to work out for me. Even though its torture, I want nothing more than to be next to Hailey the entire drive.

Allison starts us off on the alphabet game; well, at least that's what we call it. You start at the beginning of the alphabet and say a word that begins with that letter. The next person says your letter and word plus theirs, which is the next letter in the alphabet. At first it's easy, but as the game goes on, it gets harder to remember everyone's words. Allison always kicks ass at this game, which is why she is always the one to start it. We are able to make it to the letter M before Liam messes up, which kicks him out of the game. I'm out next at the letter Q. The girls decide it's not fun just the two of them, and we move on to name that tune, again our version. We are all music lovers, but Hales really likes this game. She always wins. We turn down the radio and each take turns playing a small clip of a song, while the rest of us guess the artist of the song. Liam is at a disadvantage. Driving, he only gets to guess. Allison refuses to let him participate and get distracted behind the wheel. Smart girl that one. She also lost both of her parents in a car accident. She takes that shit seriously, as she should. We all should. We all do.

Hailey starts us off. That girl always pulls deep into the archives. She makes us work for it. We all love music, but Hales is an 'I love all genres, and I can kick your ass in name that tune' kind of music lover. She thrives on stumping us. Just something else I love about her. We usually know the song and can even sing along most of the time; however, in this game you have to name the artist.

She starts to play her chosen song, and I immediately recognize it as "Your Love." "The Outfield," I blurt out. Hales looks at me and smiles.

"Why, Aiden, have you been brushing up on your artist recognition?" she asks in shock.

"You love that song," I tell her with a wink. This seems to shock her even more than me actually knowing who sings it. She opens and closes her mouth a couple times. She settles on closed as Allie declares that it's her turn. I know so much about her. I know she loves the beach. I know that when she loves something, it's with everything inside of her. I know she loves photography and the pictures she takes are amazing. I know I want her to be mine, and I can't have her.

Allison plays the clip of her song and we all laugh as we hear "Rock and Roll" by Avril Lavigne blare from her phone. Before we can get the name out, both Allison and Hailey are singing their favorite line of the song at the top of their lungs...

"I am the motherfucking princess," they both sing as loud as they can. Rocking out and shaking the Pathfinder.

Liam and I burst out laughing, both shaking our heads. They love this song and that line particularly. These girls are crazy, but we wouldn't change them for the world. God, I'm gonna miss this girl. She has become such a huge part of my life. Not seeing her every day, well...it just might kill me.

The remainder of the drive is much of the same. The girls give us a live rolling karaoke show while Liam and I laugh at their antics. I watch as Liam always has to be touching Allison. His hand on her leg, his fingers laced with hers, kissing the back of her hand. For all the shit I give him about being whipped, I'm also envious.

Liam pulls into the local grocery store, and we all climb out and stretch our legs. The girls head inside to stock up on supplies while Liam and I hang out by the car.

"Hey, man. Can I ask you a favor?" Liam asks with a serious expression on his face.

"Anything," I reply, because really, he didn't need to ask that. He knows I have his back.

"Earlier today, I heard what the girls were talking about before my tickle fest with Allie," he tells me.

I'm intrigued. He looks concerned.

"I overheard them talking about some skimpy bikini and Hales hooking up with some dude," he says as if he's pained that the words even cross his lips.

I tighten my fists at my sides. Just thinking about her with anyone else…it pisses me the fuck off. "What exactly do you need me to do?" I ask, hoping my voice doesn't reveal the anger I feel coursing through me.

"I don't know, man." Liam runs his hands across his face. "Distract her, maybe? Look, I know she's gonna meet someone, and I'm going to have to deal with it, but not like this. I don't want her first time to be some two week fling in the summer. She deserves better than that. I just want her safe."

She's still a virgin! I had my suspicions, but it isn't my place to ask those kinds of questions. "I can't stop her from hooking up," I tell him through gritted teeth. I could, oh hell yes, I could. But that would be wrong. Hales isn't mine. No matter how much I want her, I have no right to keep her from finding someone else. I chose to not act on these feelings I have for her to make sure she would always be a part of my life. Now I need to man up and accept that she'll be with someone else, and by the sound of it, a hell of a lot sooner than I was prepared to see.

Liam loudly exhales. "I know you can't stop her, but try and distract her. I know I tend to lose myself in Allie, and I'll try to not let that happen, but if you can just hang out with her, you know? Don't give her the chance to go searching for someone. Maybe we can at least protect her from a fling for her first time," his voice is desperate. I see it eating him up inside at the thought.

If he only knew what his words were doing to me. The anger coursing through my veins at the thought of my Hailey with someone else, someone who doesn't love and respect her. *Yeah, I'm pissed all right.*

I hear the girls laughing as they push their loaded down cart out of the store. Liam and I rush to them and take over, loading everything in the Pathfinder. I return the cart to the corral and slide in next to Hailey. I am sitting a little closer to the middle than I should, but I suddenly need to feel close to her. I need to get the image of her and some no-name douche bag out of my head. I swear, if anyone tries to hurt her… I shake my head, trying to clear my thoughts and calm down.

# ~ 12 ~

## Hailey

Aiden seems to be acting off. I can't really put my finger on it. I don't know what could have happened while Allie and I were in the store, but I can feel the tension coming off him in waves. He slides in, sitting a little closer than he normally does. I inch closer to him and rest my hand on his leg.

"Hey, you all right?" I whisper softly.

His stares at my hand on his leg, I start to pull away, but he places his on top of mine. He gently strokes his thumb across my knuckles. He leans down in the seat so our shoulders are touching, never taking his eyes off our hands. He releases a heavy breath. "Yeah, I'm good, angel," he whispers back.

I melt. Every damn time he calls me angel, I melt. I don't try to make conversation. I don't really want to say anything that I might regret, or that Allison and Liam can overhear. I adjust my position, rest my head on his shoulder, and close my eyes. I want to climb in his lap and demand he tell me what's wrong, but I can't. So instead, I touch him as much as I can get away with. We have a good thirty minutes until we reach the beach house, so I'll pretend to be napping until then. I feel his head rest against mine as he whispers, "Rest, angel."

My plan of pretending to sleep? Well, I did actually fall asleep. It was worth it though, because of how I am woken up. I hear Aiden whisper, "Wake up, angel. We're here." I open my eyes and see that he is close, so close. He lifts his hand and cups my cheek. "Sorry to wake you, baby, but we made it."

I nod, because, holy shit, speaking is not something that my brain can handle at the moment. Aiden has been treating me differently. The last few months we have flirted more, but he has never called me baby. And just recently he has started calling me angel. I like it a lot. Is my mind playing tricks on me? Is this really happening?

Aiden leans up and places a tender kiss on my forehead. He opens his door and climbs out, leaving me in my seat unable to speak, unable to comprehend what just happened. It feels important, like our relationship is changing. I know I tend to let my imagination wander and pretend that he wants me. Shit! I may have to break down and talk to Allison about this. I know she will be supportive. I just do not want Liam to find out. I need to talk to my best friend. I know she hates to keep anything from Liam, but surely best friend and future sister-in-law code can trump that on some things. Things like me being in love with their best friend.

I jump at the sound of knocking on my window. It's Allison. "Hey, lazy bones, let get moving," she speaks through the glass. Taking one last deep breath to calm my racing heart, I open the door and climb out.

It only takes a couple of trips to get everything unloaded. The guys carry triple what we do, so yeah, that helps. The beach house has five bedrooms. My parents have the master suite downstairs and there are four additional rooms upstairs. Liam carries all of his and Allie's things into the room he always uses. I choose the room I always claim as mine, and Aiden takes one of the spares. *I wish he was sharing with me.*

By the time we finish unpacking and fix something to eat, it's evening. Liam builds a fire in the pit. Aiden brings the chairs out of the storage shed while Allison and I stock up a cooler with beer and wine coolers, of course. The guys had bought the drinks yesterday, preparing for our trip. They even bought us our favorite "girly" drink, Grape Smirnoff. *Yum.* We carry the cooler down and place it behind one of the chairs away from the fire. Allison runs to Liam, and he catches her easily in his arms, swinging her in circles. I, however, slowly lower myself into a lounge chair watching the fire. I peer out of the corner of my eye as Aiden lowers himself in the chair next to mine. I notice that there are two chairs on the other side of the fire. I wonder if he set them up that way on purpose. GAH! I need to stop thinking that he is trying to get closer! I need to just S-T-O-P!

"Tired?" he asks softly.

"Not too bad. My catnap on the way here helped." I turn my head and smile at him.

He's staring at me, but turns his head once he realizes that he's been busted.

"They're really happy," he says, tilting his head towards Liam and Allison.

"Yeah, they really are. I'm happy for them," I say.

"Me too," he replies quietly.

Aiden and I sit in silence as we watch the fire. Liam and Allison are curled up on a lounger across from us. All of us are quiet, just enjoying the sounds of the ocean and the cracking of the fire. We remain this way for what seems like hours. Liam and Allie rise and say they are heading in for the night.

"I'm surprised they lasted this long," Aiden says, laughing softly.

I can't help but chuckle. "Me either. They held out longer than I would have." The words are out of my mouth before I can stop them. Shit. Shit. Shit. Hopefully Aiden will let it go and not try to dig deeper into the meaning of what I said.

"Do tell," he says with a smirk. He turns on his side in the lounger to face me.

Yep, so not that lucky.

I turn on my side to face him as well. "You really want to know?" I ask him.

"Yes."

My eyes find his. I feel like something monumental is happening. I just can't put my finger on it. I decide to let my word-vomit flow. I can't scare him away; he's not even mine.

"Like I said, they held out longer than I would have. I would give anything to have that kind of connection with someone. To always feel loved, safe, and secure. Knowing that at the end of the day, no matter how good or how shitty it was, that one person was there waiting to wrap his arms around me, tell me he loves me, and make love to me." I feel my face blush on that one. I'm glad that it's dark, and hopefully the glow of the fire will mask my embarrassment.

Aiden sits quietly, watching me with those chocolate eyes of his. I watch him watching me. He stands up, scoots his lounger closer to mine, and lays back down facing me. We are so close I could reach out and touch him. I don't get the chance because Aiden cups my face with the palm of his hand. He gently takes his thumb and strokes underneath my eye.

"Do you not feel safe, angel? Did someone hurt you?" he asks with a mix of concern and anger in his voice.

"No," I say in a strained voice, shaking my head. "It's not that, it's just…"

"It's what?"

"I just want to know what it feels like to be the center of someone's universe. Someone who chose me to be that person for them. Not my parents or my older brother. But someone who chooses me to share everything intimate in their life. I wish I had someone who loves me and I, in turn, love them, the way that Liam and Allison love each other, is all." I rush to get the words out to explain. "I just want that connection, to be someone's more." I must sound crazy to him.

Aiden sits up and pulls me onto his lounger and into his arms. He pulls me tight against his chest. "You are more; you deserve all of that and more. Please, don't ever settle for less."

I feel him kiss the top of my head. I snuggle deeper into his embrace. "You deserve that too, Aiden," I whisper.

"Maybe so," he says. "But you are the motherfucking princess, remember?" he says with a chuckle.

I elbow him in the ribs.

"Hey! Take it easy. I'm just messing with you." He laughs.

"Serves you right, Mister. Don't mess with me," I say, trying to hold back my laughter.

"The fire's about burnt out. Let's get you to bed," he says, releasing me from his embrace.

## ~ 13 ~

# *Aiden*

I throw the water and ice that's left in the cooler onto the fire to make sure that it's out. I then place my hand on the small of Hailey's back and lead her back to the house. Stepping into the kitchen from the patio, I stop to make sure the door is secure. I turn back and find Hailey waiting for me. The house is dark, but the moon is bright and she looks gorgeous bathed in its light. I reach my hand out to her and she takes it, lacing her fingers through mine. I gently squeeze her hand, letting her know that I'm happy she accepted. I lead her up the stairs and stop in front of her room. I wrap my arms around her and bury my face in her neck, breathing her in. "Sweet dreams, angel," I whisper. It takes more strength than I knew I had to pull away from her and continue down the hall to my room without her. It's getting harder and harder to keep my distance, to not tell her and show her how much she means to me. I'm pushing the limits of our "friendship," but I can't seem to stop myself. I'm a fucking train wreck waiting to happen.

I decide on a cold shower to wash off the day and clear my head. Unfortunately, it doesn't work. All I can think about is Hailey and those mesmerizing blue eyes, the feel of her in my arms, holding her by the fire. *Fuck!* My arms ache to hold her. This is going to be a long night. I grab my phone and headphones from the nightstand and hit my music icon. Music is always a good distraction. I select shuffle and Nickelback begins to play, so much for my distraction. I lay there and listen to "Trying Not To Love You." It's perfect really. The more I fight my attraction to her, this overwhelming need I have

65

for her, it only makes me fall faster and harder. So, what do I do? Well, I hit repeat and fall asleep thinking about Hailey and how I have tried not to love her, but failed miserably.

I wake up to the sun shining through the windows. I use the restroom, brush my teeth, throw on a t-shirt, and head downstairs. As soon as I open my bedroom door, I can smell sausage cooking. My mouth is watering. Hailey makes the best biscuits and gravy. *Please, let her be making biscuits and gravy.*

My nose leads me to the kitchen. Allie and Hales are both there, dancing around to the radio and rolling out the dough for homemade biscuits. *Yes!* "Have I told you lately that you both are amazing?" I ask them.

They both jump at the sound of my voice, but reward me with warm smiles. "Good morning," Allie says.

"Yes, we are well aware that we are amazing, but you can continue to tell us," Hales says with a wink.

My girl is flirty this morning.

"Well, you're both beyond amazing and breakfast smells delicious," I tell them.

"Did you happen to hear Liam moving around yet up there?" Allison asks me.

"Nope," I say, pouring myself a cup of coffee. "How the hell did you manage to slip away from him?" I ask her. I really want to know. Very rarely do you see one without the other, at least not just hanging around the house.

Allison blushes.

Hailey bumps her hip into Allie's. "She wore the guy out last night." She laughs.

Allison is now crimson. Before she can respond, Liam enters the room and heads straight for his girl.

"You left me, baby," he says as he softly kisses her good morning. I turn my head to allow them some privacy, and my eyes meet with Hales's. She was watching me watch them. She offers me a small shy smile and I wink at her.

Last night lying in bed, I came to the conclusion that I need to be flirty friend Aiden at all times. I cannot let us share any more intimate moments like last night by the fire. Nope, no way. The only way I'm going to be able to keep my sanity in her presence is to fight my heart and be the friend that she has always known me to be. Yep, it's totally going to suck ass, but I can't take the chance of acting on these feelings and losing her.

"Breakfast was great! Thank you so much," I tell the girls.

"I'm glad you feel that way, Emerson," Hailey says sweetly. "You and big bro get to clean the kitchen while we go and get our suits on. We have a beach calling our name," she informs us.

Allison raises her hand for a high five. "Good plan, my bestie," she tells Hailey.

The girls disappear up the stairs, laughing the entire way. I can't help but smile at seeing them both so happy and carefree. If things were to not work out with Hales and me, this would not be the case. This morning reinforces my decision, even though it's going to be one of the hardest things I have ever had to do.

Liam and I make quick work of cleaning the kitchen. The girls appear just as we are finishing up. They bounce down the stairs and out the door, headed straight for the beach. Like the lovesick fools that we are, we grab our towels, Liam grabs the cooler and I pick up four of the smaller beach chairs from the storage cabinet on the deck, and follow them.

The MacCoy's house is nestled at the end of what they call Beach Row. The beach dead ends into a mass of rocks and a cliff. This makes it nice for us, as not many people make it this far down the beach.

Once we reach the spot the girls have chosen, I begin setting up the four chairs while Liam places the cooler underneath the canopy the girls brought down. Once I have the chairs set up, I turn around, and what I see just about makes me swallow my fucking tongue. I turn just in time to see Hailey raise her arms and pull off the black cover thingy that she had on over her suit. No scratch that; she had on over her scraps of material she is trying to pass off as a suit. *Holy fucking shit!* Hailey is wearing a barely there blue bikini. It's the same exact color of her emerald blue eyes. I can't take my eyes off her. I take my time, letting my eyes roam every inch of her. Once I reach her face, I see that she is staring right at me. Her blue eyes are sparkling and there is a hint of a smile on her lips. Those lips. Hales has lips of an angel, so soft and sweet. I feel myself getting hard and I know if I don't stop staring at her, there will be no hiding how much I want her. Liam will so kick my ass.

I feel a hard smack to the back of my head. "That's my little sister, fuckstick!" Liam says.

Rubbing the back of my head, I explain, "Yes, but she is not little anymore and she's fucking gorgeous." The words are out of my mouth before I realize what I said. Oops, I need to be more careful.

"Yes, she is," is all he says in reply. However, he is looking at me trying to figure out if there is a hidden meaning behind my words. If he only knew.

"Hales, what the fuck are you wearing? You need to go change," Liam barks at her.

"Uh, no! Not happening. I bought this for this trip and you are not dad. You don't get to tell me what to do. I will be twenty next week."

Liam mumbles to himself something about stubborn females.

I laugh as I turn my back to Hales, because I have no other choice. I need to get myself in check. This leaves me facing Allie. She smiles at me and winks. Yep, she is totally onto me. I hope she can keep it quiet. Allie pulls her shirt off also and has the same fucking bikini on as Hales. Except hers is green, the same green as her eyes. These two are going to be the death of me. I hear Liam growl behind me and my face breaks out into a huge grin. This is going to be fun.

"Hell, no! You can't wear that out here, beautiful." He is trying to be nice, but I can hear the anger in his voice just waiting to be unleashed.

Allison smiles sweetly and pats his arm. "Sure I can. Hales and I bought these just for this trip." She tries to act all innocent, but she knew that Liam would go nuts.

Liam wraps his arms around her as if he is trying to shield her from the world. "Baby, I won't be able to handle other guys seeing you in this…this thing you call a suit," he whines.

Allison smiles and places her hand on his cheek. "It doesn't matter; I only have eyes for my fiancé."

Liam pulls her tight and crushes his lips to hers. I feel Hailey step beside me. "Catastrophe averted," she says, laughing.

Without thinking, I reach out, put my arm around her waist, and pull her against my side. I bend down and whisper in her ear. "What are we gonna do with the two of you?" I ask her. She laughs and I tickle her side.

Hailey twists and turns to get away from me, and then takes off for the water. I hear Liam laugh and I turn to look at them. "What?"

"She's a handful, that's what." He laughs.

"Oh really?" Allison asks.

"Yes, really," he counters.

"Well then." Allison wiggles out of his arms and takes off running after Hailey.

Liam just stands there shaking his head, with a huge smile on his face. "That's my future wife," he tells me.

I laugh. Liam has changed so much since meeting Allison. Dude is whipped.

## ~ 14 ~

# Hailey

I wiggle out of Aiden's arms and take off running for the water. I have to get away, get some distance. When he pulled me into his arms, it took everything I have in me to remain standing. Aiden does that to me, makes me weak in the knees. I make it to the water and dive straight in. The water is warm and inviting. I love the ocean, being on the beach.

I surface and see Allison has joined me. "Those two are ridiculous," she says, laughing. "They know we don't want anyone but them. Can they not cool the alpha male bit?"

My mouth drops open and I can't speak. I know Allison has suspected that I have feelings for Aiden for a while now, but she said Aiden knows. *Shit!*

Allison is still laughing; this time, it's at me, not with me. "You seriously thought I didn't know? Hales, you are my best friend, of course I know."

"But you said *they* know. Aiden can't find out," I plead with her.

"Relax. It was more for your benefit; I just wanted you to admit that you like him. My plan was flawless," she says with a wink.

Ugh. "Please don't say anything to Liam or Aiden. I know he doesn't feel the same and I have to get over this, but..." I stop myself before I divulge too much information.

"But?" Allies prods me.

"I more than like him." I raise my head to look her in the eyes. "I love him, Allie. I have for a while now, and I know that I need to get over this, but I just can't. I am dreading when you all leave for Charlotte and leave me here, but really, I think it might help me. I need to move on, and being with him all the time makes it pretty much impossible," I tell her.

"What makes you think he doesn't feel the same way?" she counters.

"Come on, Allison. I am his best friend's little sister. He's always taken the big brother role right along with Liam. I like how we all hang out all the time and get along so well. If Aiden were to find out that I have feelings for him, that will all change. I don't want things to change."

"Change is not always bad. What if he does feel the same? The two of you could have what Liam and I have."

Poor Allison. She is living in a world of blissful happiness with my brother. Her vision is clouded by the blanket of love that Liam surrounds her in. "Trust me, okay? It has to be this way. Distance will help me get over him and move on. I can't lose what we all have. The three of you are important and I love how everything comes so easy for all of us. I'll work through this, just please don't say anything," I beg her with my eyes to understand where I'm coming from.

"Oh, all right. I won't say anything, but let it go on record in that stubborn head of yours that I think you are making a big mistake," she chastises me.

"Noted," I say, and hope that this is the end of our conversation regarding my feelings for Aiden.

Allison and I swim and splash around in the ocean until we decide that we are pruned enough. We make our way back up the beach and settle in our seats beside the guys. Liam immediately wraps a towel around Allison's arms and throws his over top of her as well. She laughs at him and throws it back at him. He growls. This earns him a laugh from all three of us.

Liam and Allison are now both on one lounger with a towel covering them. I have to hand it to my big brother, that is a creative way to get what you want. Allison can never really say no to him, nor he to her. I lie back on the lounger and decide to soak up some rays and dry out a little. I hear a low growl from beside me. I look over to find Aiden staring at me with his jaw clenched. "What?" I ask him. I have no idea what his issue is.

Aiden leans in close, bringing his lips to my ear. I am so distracted by his nearness that I miss the fact that his hand is inching towards my breast. "You need to pay closer attention, angel," he whispers as he gently pulls my bikini into place. Apparently, I was on the verge of a major nip slip.

I feel my face blush with embarrassment that Aiden was the one to notice, and fix it! He kisses my temple and sits back on his lounger as if nothing happened. My body is still humming with the electricity of his touch. Good God, he is a sexy beast. The way his fingers brushed against my breast, it almost felt deliberate. I know that's not the case; he was just helping me. Preventing me from major embarrassment and from my brother catching the show. EWWW!

I lie still and focus on breathing. I can feel the crashing beat of my heart in my chest. My chest, that is now fully covered, rapidly rises and falls with every breath. I can feel him. I want him. I feel hot tears burn the back of my eyes, and I squeeze them tight. I can't let them see this. I'm an emotional mess when it comes to Aiden, my brother's best friend. Distance, I need a little distance to get myself in check. I jump from my lounger and quickly wrap my towel around me so that I'm covered. I feel Aiden's eyes boring into me.

"What's wrong, angel?" he asks concerned.

"Nothing, I just need to use the restroom," I say. I'm already walking back towards the house.

I run up the steps and throw open the backdoor. I dash up the stairs and into my room, throwing myself on the bed. I let the tears fall. Tears of sadness that he will never be mine and tears of frustration that I can't get my shit together when he's around.

I hear a soft knock on my door. "Hales, it's me, Allison."

"It's open," I call back to her, my voice rough with emotion.

"Hales, what happened? What's wrong? You've been up here for a while now."

I bury my face in the pillow and shake my head at her.

Allison climbs up on the bed and wraps her arms around me. "It's just between us, I promise."

Letting her words sink in, I roll over and face her. I tell her about my nip slip adventure and how I let my feelings for Aiden get the best of me. "It's getting harder and harder for me to keep myself in check," I tell her.

Allison shrugs her shoulders. "Then don't."

"Are you crazy? Not only does he still see me only as Liam's little sister, Liam would so kick his ass." Has she lost her ever lovin' mind?

"You let me take care of your brother." She wags her eyebrows at me. "As for Aiden, I'm not so sure you're right. I think he sees you just fine as the woman you've become. I think it's eating at him just as much as it's eating at you."

"Seriously, Allie. You and Liam are trapped in this happy little love bubble. Don't get me wrong, I love you guys together and I am super stoked that you are going to be my sister, but not everyone finds the fairytale."

"Care to make a wager?" she goads me.

Ugh! This is a game we play often. Neither one of us can back down from a bet. I remember I bet her that she and Liam were going to be great together, and I was right. Too bad Allie is going to be going 0 for 2. "What are the stakes?" I ask her.

"Easy. I win, I get to be maid of honor at your wedding. You win, and you get free reign to plan anything you want for my bridal shower."

"First of all, regardless of who I marry, you will be my maid of honor. Second, Liam will shut an 'anything goes' bridal shower down, and you know it."

"Fine, so maybe you're right. Let's see…" Allison taps her index finger against her chin, deep in thought. "Well, we can always resort to old faithful, a day at the spa."

"Deal." I reach my hand out to her. We shake on it. I kind of feel bad that she'll have to treat me to another spa day, but oh well. A deal is a deal.

"Come on, let's head back down to the beach. The guys went to grab some pizza."

Allison and I are both in a lounger soaking up the sun when a football lands between us, scaring us both.

"Hey, sorry about that." I raise my head to put a face to the sexy voice.

"No problem," Allison says to him.

"I'm Seth. My buddies and I are here on vacation. How about you ladies?" he asks.

"We come here every summer. My parents own a beach house," I tell him. I see a group of guys waiting for him down the beach.

"Cool. Hey, you guys up for a game? We'll take it easy on you." He winks at me.

I look at Allison to gauge her reaction. She's smiling, that's a good sign. "Allie?"

"Sure. My fiancé and his best friend just went for some pizza, so we have a little while before they're back," she says sweetly.

"Fiancé? He's a lucky guy. How about you? You have a fiancé too?" he asks.

"Nope." I keep my answer short and sweet, because really, what else is there to say. I don't want to sound desperate or anything.

"Well, come on then. I'm sorry, I didn't catch your names," Seth inquires.

"I'm Hailey and this is Allison. Her fiancé is my older brother." I'm not sure why I feel the need to tell him that, but I do.

We follow Seth a little ways down the beach, and he introduces us to his friends. "Allison and Hailey, I would like for you to meet, Craig, Brian, and Scott."

*Holy yum!* These guys are huge, muscles bulging from everywhere, and they're H-O-T! I feel Allison link her arm through mine.

"It's nice to meet you. Where are you all from?" she asks sweetly.

"Ohio," one of them answers, I think he's the one Seth referred to as Scott.

"Cool," Allison replies.

"Yeah, we're seniors there. We all four play for the Buckeyes football team," Brian brags.

"Yep, Seth here is in line for the draft next year," Craig tells us.

Of course, neither Allison nor I are very impressed with this. Our men have already made it to the NFL.

"You ladies familiar with the draft?" Seth asks.

Allison and I both laugh. "Yeah, we're familiar," she tells them.

"Well, all right then. You all ready to play a little football?"

Allison's cell phone rings, stopping us all. "Hey, baby," she says in greeting.

I am watching her to see what she tells Liam. He is so not going to be impressed with this.

"Yeah, Hales and I met a few people on the beach and are getting ready to play a game of football." She winks at me. "We are just down from the house, we'll wait on you. Okay, love you too."

"Sorry, guys, my fiancé is back with dinner. Maybe next time," she says sweetly.

Seth puts his arm around me. It's a gesture that friends would do, but he is not my friend. I just met the guy. I'm just about ready to tell him that I need to head back with Allison when I hear Aiden answer for me. *Aiden!*

# ~ 15 ~

# Aiden

When we get back to the house, the girls are nowhere to be found. Liam calls Allie to see where they ran off to.

"Hey, beautiful girl, where are you?" he asks her.

I see his face go red with anger. *What the fuck is going on?*

"Stay there, we're on our way. I mean it, don't move, Allison. I love you." He ends the call on his cell and shoves it back into his pocket.

"What the hell was that about?" I ask, worried. He never talks to Allison like that.

"Apparently the girls met a few guys on the beach who convinced them to play a friendly game of football," he seethes.

"What! They know better than that. They don't even know these jackoffs!" I say, barely controlling my own anger.

"My thoughts exactly. Allison was acting all nonchalant about it. Like it's no big fucking deal that my fiancé and little sister are going to be mauled by a bunch of half-naked wanna-be football players."

Liam flies out the patio doors and down the back deck. I'm right on his heels. We reach the group and stop right behind the girls. We're there just long enough for one of the cocksuckers to put his arm around Hailey, and my eyes blur from the red-hot rage that flares through me. Who the fuck does he think he is? Touching what's mine!

I step up close to Hales. "I would appreciate it if you would remove your hands from my girl," I say through gritted teeth. The guy must hear my anger and know I'm not messing around, because he drops his arm. I immediately pull Hailey's back against my chest and wrap my arms around her waist. I kiss her temple. She's safe. What these girls were thinking, I have no idea.

"Sorry, man," Seth says, raising his arms. "Allison said she was engaged, but Hailey didn't mention a boyfriend," he says, trying to calm me.

Hailey starts to speak, "He's…" I nuzzle her neck, hoping to distract her.

It works.

"Well, now you know," I say, not giving a shit that I sound like a possessive asshole.

I hold Hailey even tighter. She has to feel my heart beating against her back. I feel like it's about to beat out of my chest.

Allison tries to break the tension with small talk. "Babe, this is Seth, Brian, Craig, and Scott. They're all seniors at OSU. They play football," she tells him.

"Really?" Liam asks. He's still pissed and has the same death grip on Allison as I do on Hailey.

Allison simply smiles up at him. "Yeah, they were just telling us that they are in line for the draft next year."

"Well, not all of us," Craig says. "Just Seth here. Rumored to be first round," he says cockily. "You guys ever play?" he asks us.

I can't help it, I laugh out loud at that one. "Yeah, we've played," I say, bumping my shoulder into Liam's. We're standing side by side with our girls in our arms where they belong.

One of the guys, I think they said his name was Brian, makes the connection. I can see it in his eyes as soon as he does. He looks back and forth from me to Liam with his mouth hanging open. Honestly, I would find this entire situation amusing as hell and probably would have already introduced myself and made it easier for

78

them, but no, they were honing in on my girl. I'm so not making it easy.

"Holy shit! You're Aiden Emerson and you," he turns towards Liam "you're Liam MacCoy. Dude, congrats on the draft," Brian tells us.

Liam nods his head in recognition. I, on the other hand, make a point to pull Hailey tighter against my chest. I kiss the top of her head. I need him to know, need all of these ass wipes to know, that Hales is off limits. I'm actually surprised Liam is as calm as he is, but then again, Allison wasn't being mauled when we walked up either. It was also obvious that Allison let them know that she was taken. Not that they couldn't see the huge diamond on her finger.

Just like that, it hits me like the waves crashing on the beach. Hailey isn't mine and she *is* available. What if she ends up dating one of these douche bags? I pull a deep breath into my lungs. I want Hailey with an intensity that I have never known, but I continue to fight this battle I have staged in my head on the daily. I'm beginning to wonder if I should just throw caution to the wind, and beg her to be mine. Then I think about losing her. What if we really are just better off as friends? Would I be able to stand by and let her be with someone else after she's been mine? I don't even need to think about the answer, it's a big hell to the no. I can't let things change with us. I'm willing to sacrifice my heart just to be able to be with her. If I wasn't sure before, the emotion is now cemented deep within my soul. I'm in love with Hailey MacCoy. *Fuck me!*

"So how about it? You guys up for a friendly game?" Craig asks. I think it's Craig. I really didn't pay much attention to the introductions.

"We'd love to, but the girls' food is getting cold. Maybe we'll catch up with you guys later," Liam says. I can still tell he is not impressed with the situation.

"Cool. Well, it was nice to meet you all," Seth says, and with that, they turn and walk the opposite way on the beach.

Liam and Allison turn to head towards the house. I know I should follow them, but damn it, I'm holding her and I don't want to let go. She stands still in my arms, not trying to break our connection. My right arm is still draped across her waist holding her tight against my chest. I softly grip her left hip and turn her to face me. She's staring straight at my chest, not meeting my eyes. I gently lift her chin with my index finger. Fuck, she is so beautiful. What if something would have happened to her today? I can feel the anger trying to resurface. I take a deep breath and exhale slowly. Hailey is silently watching me now. I lean down and rest my forehead against hers and close my eyes. Both of my hands find her hips. I'm going to take every advantage to touch her that I can.

"I was worried about you, angel," I tell her honestly. Well, as honest as I can be.

"Aiden, we were fine. Those guys were just being friendly."

"You don't know them. Hell, they could have taken you both and did God only knows what to you." I swallow back the emotion caused by just the thought of her being hurt.

"I'm not yours to worry about," she whispers.

And there it is, the knife that is twisting in my chest. She's right. I know it and she knows it, but fuck if I like it.

I pull back and bring both of my hands to her cheeks. "Angel, I care about you. You may not be mine, but I will never let anything happen to you. Do you understand that?" I ask her. I really need her to know how special she is.

"One big brother is enough, Aiden. You don't have to feel obligated to protect me."

"Who said I wanted to be your big brother?" I ask, trying to keep my voice calm. This is truly a daunting feat with all of the rage boiling inside me. She thinks I want to be her big brother? *Fuck that!*

"Don't you? Why else would you go all alpha Aiden and try to keep me from them?" she asks me.

I watch her closely as she waits for my answer. This beautiful girl has no idea of the war I have fought these past few months. She has no idea how she affects me, how much I want her. This is killing me. Wanting something this much, something that I can't have. She licks her lips and now all I can think about is tasting her. I don't even realize that I'm going to do it until our lips meet and I'm consumed with her sweetness. Lips of an angel, I tell you.

I move one hand behind her neck and the other is holding her cheek. I angle her head back and deepen the kiss. Hailey opens her mouth and I take full advantage to slide my tongue in, and hers immediately duals with mine. She moans and my desire is fueled. I can't get her close enough, can't get enough period. Hailey slows the kiss and pulls her lips from mine. I tug her into a tight embrace.

"I need for you to always be safe. Not because I feel like your older brother, but because you are important to me. I couldn't handle it if something happened to you."

I feel her nod against my chest. "Let's go. They're going to wonder where we are," I say against her ear.

She slowly pulls away from me. "Thank you, Aiden." With that, she turns and heads back to the beach house.

I stand there and watch my heart walk away from me. I place my hand over my heart and rub the ache that is throbbing in my chest. No girl will ever mean to me what Hailey MacCoy does.

## ~ 16 ~

## *Hailey*

I turn on shaky legs and walk back to the beach house. Putting all of my concentration into not letting Aiden see how much I'm affected by him. That kiss...it was different than any other kiss we have shared up to this point. It was filled with passion, desire, and need. I know I feel all of those things when it comes to Aiden, and gauging by his reaction and the look in his eyes, he feels the same for me.

I'm trying to wrap my head around the fact that Aiden wants me. Well, maybe not want as in the forever kind of want. I do believe him though, when he tells me that he would protect me and wants me safe. I could tell by the look in his eyes that he was being sincere. He says I'm important to him, and I believe that too. What this means for us, I have no clue. I'm not holding out for more, because I just don't see that happening for us. There is a part of me, even though it's a small part, that is starting to admit that things between Aiden and I are changing. We both acknowledge that there is a connection. Now we just need to decide what we are going to do with it.

By the time I reach the beach house, my legs are more stable and I seem to have a handle on my emotions. I join Liam and Allison on the deck and to my surprise, Aiden is right behind me.

"What took you guys so long?" Liam questions, eyeing us closely.

"I was just reminding Hailey, to be careful." He looks at Allison. "Both of you need to be careful. You can't trust just anyone these days."

Liam nods his head in agreement. "I told Allie the same thing. We just need you guys to be safe. Especially you," he says, pointing to me. "In a few short weeks, the three of us will be in Charlotte and you will be here without us to look out for you. I need you to promise me that you will make good decisions and be safe."

"I know, Liam. I love you for it, I really do. But how am I supposed to meet new people, and move on from losing my three best friends, if I can't even talk to other people," I say with a sigh.

"I didn't say you can't talk to people. I said be careful. Today was a risk. The two of you were alone with four big guys who could easily over power you. Make sure you don't find yourself alone in that type of situation. If you meet a guy, meet him out in public or with a group from school before you put all your trust in him." Liam runs his fingers through his hair. He glances over at Aiden before turning his attention back to me.

"I know you are going to date, and one day you will meet someone that loves you like I love Allie. I want that for you. I also don't want you to settle or end up with some douche bag that doesn't treat you like you deserve. Just be careful, okay?"

I walk around the table to stand behind Liam and wrap my arms around his neck. "I love you, big brother. I promise to be safe."

I stand up and walk back to my seat. I take a minute to look at each of them before I say. "I love all three of you, and I'm going to miss you like crazy."

Allison clears her throat. "Well then, we need to enjoy our time here together. Who knows how long it will be until we can do this again. And, somebody has a birthday in two days." She winks at me.

"Yeah, what do you have in mind, Hales?" Liam asks me.

"Really, just hanging out is fine. Sitting by the fire, maybe a wine cooler or two," I say sweetly.

"I think that can be arranged," he says.

84

With that, we all dig into the pizza. Pizza that thankfully, due to the summer heat, is not as cold as I would have guessed.

The next two days consisted of lounging on the beach and just hanging out. Aiden and I have been able to act as though the "incident" two days ago never happened. Well, at least that's what I'm telling myself. I think about it all the time, the kiss, his declaration that I'm important to him, and not just because I'm Liam's little sister. To be quite honest, my nerves are shot.

Today is my birthday. I'm twenty years old. I need to let loose and have some fun, and I intend to do just that. I plan to get Allison on my side, so that she can run interference with Liam and Aiden. I leave my bedroom in search of Allison. I find her in the laundry room.

"Hey, you," I say as I hop up on the dryer. "Need any help?"

"Hey, no I'm good, but thanks," she replies. "What's up?" she asks, shutting the door on the washing machine.

I shrug my shoulders. "Well, I actually wanted to talk to you about something."

Allison hops up on the washer. "I'm all ears."

"Well, you know how Liam and Aiden have been stuck to us like glue since the run in with Seth and his friends the other day?"

Allison rolls her eyes. "Yeah."

"Well, I really just want to let loose tonight. I was hoping you could help run interference with them. I'm good with it just being us, but I'm seeing lots of alcohol in my near future. I just want to relax. I feel like I'm always on edge anymore."

"You know I have your back. I assume the stress is a multitude of things. Including your feelings for Aiden?"

I stare straight ahead at the wall. "Yeah, that has a lot to do with it."

"Hales, I really think …"

"Please, Allie. Just don't go there, okay? It's not going to happen. Can we please just kick back and have fun, like old times? Before I let my heart take over my mind?" I plead.

Allison releases a deep sigh. "Yes, let's get our drink on. Don't worry about the guys, I'll talk to both of them. This is your day."

We hop off the washer and dryer at the same time and I engulf her in a hug. "What am I going to do without you? I'm going to miss this so much," I say, fighting against tears.

"We're just going to be a few hours away. Everything will work out, you'll see," she tells me.

That's Allison. Always looking at the positive side of life. She's been through so much loss, and yet she still manages to make lemonade out of lemons. Liam really lucked out with finding her, we all did.

Allison and I make our way to the living room to find Liam and Aiden sprawled out on either couch. Allison runs and jumps on top of Liam and he engulfs her and pulls her tight. I stand awkwardly for a few minutes, and then head to the recliner in the corner. As I am walking past the couch Aiden is laying on, he lifts his feet and motions with his head for me to sit. This is something that we have done a million times, but now it seems…more intimate. I want it to be more intimate. I sit down and he rests his feet in my lap.

"What are you two up to?" he asks me.

"Nothing really. Allie was doing laundry and I was keeping her company," I tell him.

"Today's the big day. You feel any older?"

I shake my head. "No, not really."

"What do you want to do today, birthday girl?"

Allison speaks up. "Hales and I are going to, as you boys say, tie one on tonight," she says. I didn't even think that she was paying any attention to us.

This statement, of course, gets Liam's attention. "What? Baby, I don't think that's a good idea."

Allison sits up and gives Liam the look. You know, the one that tells him he needs to shut the hell up and give her her way. Yeah, that look. "I said that Hailey and I are going to tie one on, get our drink on, hammer down, whatever you want to call it. She and I only have a few more weeks together, and we are going to celebrate her birthday by getting wasted. You, my wonderful fiancé, and you, my brother, are going to make sure we stay out of trouble. You will provide us with our alcohol of choice and, if needed, hold our hair as we are praying to the porcelain gods," she says, still giving Liam "the look," daring him to object.

I watch as my brother opens and closes his mouth, no words coming across his lips. Allison has stunned him speechless. I love my best friend, my sister. She's knows how much I need this, how much I just need to relax and let loose, and she is making sure that Liam and Aiden don't get in the way of that.

Aiden nudges my leg with his foot. "Is that what you want, angel?" he asks softly.

I shake my head yes. "I need to let loose. I want to do it where I know I'll be safe. I want to party with my best friends, before you all leave me."

Aiden clenches his jaw. "You will be safe. You deserve to let loose and have fun."

Liam stands up from the couch. "Let's head to the store and get what they want and get this night over with." He drops a kiss on Allison's head and walks out the door. Aiden stands to follow him.

"Any requests, birthday girl?" he asks me.

"Not really. Just surprise me, and bring a lot." I smile sweetly. He shakes his head and smiles as he follows out the door after Liam.

# ~ 17 ~

# *Aiden*

Liam and I are in the Pathfinder and headed towards the local liquor store. I can't help but wonder what's up with those two. Allison is not a big drinker, and Hailey really isn't either. I could understand if this was her twenty-first birthday, but it's not. Today is number twenty. I smile remembering a fourteen-year-old Hailey. She was pretty then, but now...now she's a goddess. I shift in my seat to adjust the hard on that is starting to appear.

"What's gotten into those two?" Liam asks me, reading my thoughts.

I shrug my shoulders. "I can only assume it's what they said. Allison will be leaving with us in a few weeks, and Hailey will be without us in Chapel Hill. No, it's not that far, but they are used to being together all the time, every day. We all are," I tell him.

Liam sighs. "I guess so. Listen man, you have to help me tonight. I assume it's just going to be the four of us, but I can't watch both of them. Can you please keep a close eye on Hales?"

I swallow the lump in my throat. "Yeah, man. I got Hales covered. She'll be with me." My heart and body are screaming yes. They both crave time with Hales. My mind on the other hand knows that this is not going to help my growing affection for her. I need to keep myself sober, so things don't get carried away. If we are both wasted, who knows what could happen.

Liam pulls into the lot and turns off the ignition. "I forgot to ask what they wanted," he says solemnly.

"I asked Hales, she said to surprise her, but to buy a lot," I tell him.

He groans and opens his door. Once in the liquor store, the possibilities are endless. The girls are not seasoned drinkers, so the heavy stuff is out of the question.

Liam decides on amaretto sour, strawberry daiquiri, and some flavored Smirnoff coolers. I question mixing alcohol but he shrugs it off, saying that none of it is too hard, and that he and I will be mixing the drinks, so they won't be strong. *Good angle, MacCoy.*

Our next stop is the grocery store. Steaks, baked potatoes, and salad. I choose a white cake with whipped icing from the bakery and have them put "Happy Birthday, Hales" in pink, her favorite color. We also pick up some supplies to make ice cream sundaes, another of her favorites.

Arriving back at the house, we pack in all of the supplies and put them away. The girls left us a note on the counter saying that they are on the beach. Shit! I bet there are tons of jackasses mulling around them. Liam reads the note first, and then hands it to me. Neither of us say anything. We just run up the stairs to our rooms, slide into board shorts, and rush out the door. No words are needed. We both know what we are going to find. Allie and Hales are gorgeous; no man in his right mind could walk by and not notice.

Sure enough, as we get closer to the beach, the girls are sitting on lounger chairs surrounded by Seth, Scott, Brian, and Craig. Did these fuckers not get the message yesterday? I clinch my fists tight to my sides, and hear Liam growl next to me. We step up behind the girls' chairs. Liam slides in behind Allison and pulls her to his chest. Without giving it another thought, I do the same with Hales. I kiss her temple once I have her close to me. "I missed you, angel," I whisper in her ear, loud enough that Seth, the fucker who is kneeling beside her, can hear me. I don't even acknowledge him. If I do, I'll have to hit him, and that will make Hales mad. I don't want her mad at me on her birthday of all days.

Hailey scoots her ass back, right against my crotch. This tells me that she's not interested in Seth. Did he try something? Did he do something to make her uncomfortable? I move my face so I can whisper in her other ear, in hopes that Seth can't hear me.

"Are you okay, angel? Did he hurt you? Hurt Allison?" I whisper softly. Trying to keep myself calm, I pray that she tells me no. Otherwise, Seth is about to be worked over, and I'm about to be benched with the NFL before I even take the field. I know this because I won't stop if he did something to either of them. It's gonna take an army to get me off him.

Don't. Fuck. With. My. Girls.

She shakes her head no and I can feel myself relax. She turns to look at me over her shoulder and her eyes find mine. I lean my ear down to her lips.

"I'm just not interested and he doesn't seem to get it," she whispers.

I relax even more, knowing she doesn't want him. I pull her back to rest flat against my chest and rest my head on her shoulder. I feel her shiver at the contact of my breath on her neck. I'm glad to know that she's affected too. If she only knew how she affects me. Well, she probably does by now. I'm hard as a rock, with her ass resting right on top of me. The lines keep getting blurred from what I want and what I know needs to happen. I can't think of a time in my life when I have wanted anything as bad as I want Hailey.

After several lame attempts at small talk, Seth and his posse say their goodbyes and head back down the beach. Even though I don't want them around either of the girls, I'm sad to see them go. This means I have to let Hailey go. I won't be able to hold her in my arms and nuzzle her neck. *Fuck my life!*

I again find myself in the position of having to let her go. I hate letting her go. As if she is in my head, Hailey moves away from me, scooting to sit on the edge of the lounger.

"We can't leave you two alone for all the damn vultures," Liam says.

Allison laughs. "Babe, we were fine. They were just being friendly. We knew you were going to be home soon. We actually told the guys you were in the house. They didn't even know we were here alone," she tells him.

"Fuck, and they were still all up on you," he says.

"I'm hungry, what did you bring for the birthday girl's dinner?" Allison asks, changing the subject.

"Steak, baked potato, and salad." Liam stands and pulls Allison up with him. "I'll start the grill."

I watch as they walk away. Reaching over, I grab Hailey's hand, and lace our fingers together. Gently, I rub my thumb across her knuckles, just needing to touch her. I look up to find her gaze locked on our hands. Pulling her hand to my lips, her eyes following me, and I place a soft kiss on her palm. I lace my fingers back through hers and stand up, pulling her with me. After gathering her things, and we head back to the house with our hands still laced, still connected.

We reach the steps that lead to the deck and I gently squeeze her hand before releasing it. She offers me a shy smile and I want to taste those lips. I hate that I have to let her go. She seems to understand because she bumps her shoulder with mine and starts up the stairs. I watch her go, my body aching with desire for her.

Liam mans the grill, Allison makes the salads, and I mix the girls their first drink. Hailey is sitting on the deck. We all three have instructed her to not lift a finger. She didn't protest.

I bring Hales and Allison their first drink of the night, Strawberry daiquiris, on the weak side of course. Dinner is great. Nothing beats a good grilled steak with baked potato. Allison suggests we play spoons. She loves that damn game.

Hailey, of course, is on board. She jets off to the kitchen to gather three spoons and a deck of cards to set up the game.

The beach house has outdoor speakers that are connected to the entertainment center in the living room. Liam goes in and sets his iPod to shuffle. He and Hailey return at the same time, both wearing huge smiles. Who am I kidding? We all love this damn game.

We play the first round and Allison gets a letter. The girls announce that they need a refill so I head to the kitchen and make them another drink. I grab two bottles of water out of the fridge. I deliver the drinks, handing Liam the second bottle of water. He nods his head and that's all the confirmation that I need to know that he and I are on the same page. *Must stay sober!*

We continue on with the game, and as always, we are all enjoying ourselves. Allison and Hailey have had a few more refills and both are relaxed. So relaxed, that everything is suddenly funny to them. I lost the last round bringing to the tally of S-P-O-O. This the girls find hilarious.

"Ace is a SPOO." Allison laughs.

"I'm a SPO!" Hailey cheers. "You're going down, Emerson," she says, pointing her finger at me.

"Bring it, angel," I say. If she only knew what else I want her to bring.

The next few rounds go quickly. Allison and Hailey are the dealers, and it appears that the cards didn't get shuffled as well as they should have. Alcohol does that. Allison ends up being the first one out.

Hailey pouts. "I can't play without my bestie. New game," she tells us.

"Let's dance," Allison shouts. "Baby, I need a refill," she tells Liam as she tilts her cup up and finishes off her last drink.

"Me too," Hailey says loudly.

Liam shakes his head and smiles as he walks away. He comes back with two bottles of Smirnoff and two more bottles of water.

Allison and Hailey click their bottles together as they grind to the music. Liam sits down next to me and we watch them. They are both well past their way to "tying one on" as Allison called it.

"It's good to see them like this. Happy and carefree," he says.

"Listen, man, I know I give you shit, but Allie has changed since she met you. She's open to life and new possibilities. I've never seen her this happy. I have you to thank for that."

"Don't thank me for loving her. She's the best thing that has ever happened to me. Loving her is easy."

We both sit quietly for what seems like forever, just watching the girls dance and laugh.

"I still can't believe she's going to be my wife," Liam says out of the blue.

I laugh. "Yeah, I never thought I would see the day that Liam MacCoy settled down," I chide him.

"Just wait, dude, when you find it, you'll understand."

I don't say anything to that, because well...I have a feeling I may have found the one that could get me to change my way of thinking, but I won't let myself have her. My eyes find Hailey as they always do, and I take in her movements, her laughter. I love to hear her laugh.

The next song is a slow one, "Can't Fight This Feeling" by REO Speedwagon. Liam jumps up and makes his way to Allison, pulling her into his arms. I watch them, wishing it was Hales and me.

"Don't leave me hanging, Emerson," I hear her say.

I look up to find her standing there with her hand held out, waiting for me.

I reach out and take her hand, tugging her close. She wraps her hands around my neck and begins running her fingers through my hair. I place my arms around her waist and pull her as tight as I can get her. I glance over her shoulder and see that Liam and Allison are in there own little world. Good, that means there is less of a chance of them witnessing this. I told myself that I would keep my distance, but I can't. I will never be able to turn her away, tell her no.

Hailey brings her arms down and places them around my waist, hugging me close as she rests her head against my chest. I lean down and kiss the top of her head, and try like hell to memorize every minute, every single fucking second, of what it feels like to have her in my arms.

This song, fuck me, it's perfect for us, for me. I sing softly in her ear, hoping she understands what I'm trying to say.

The song ends and Hailey slowly lifts her head from my chest. "Thanks for the dance," she whispers as she leans up and kisses my cheek. I release her from my hold and she stumbles a bit. I would love to think that it's my effect on her, but I'm pretty sure it's the alcohol.

I reach out and catch her with my arms, helping her regain her balance.

"Looks like she's had enough too," Liam says as he steps up beside us.

"Yeah, I think you're right." My voice is thick with emotion. I pray that he doesn't notice.

"I'm taking Allie to bed. Can you make sure Hales gets settled in?"

"Sure, man. I'll see you guys in the morning," I tell him.

Liam scoops Allison up in his arms and carries her into the house.

Hailey falls against my chest, losing her balance once again. I wrap my arms around her. I can't seem to control myself where she's concerned.

"I can't feel my legs," she mumbles against my chest.

I kiss the top of her head. "I got you, angel," I say, bending down and scooping her up in my arms. I carry her in the house and set her on the couch. I run back to the door, closing and locking it.

I find Hailey where I left her, eyes closed breathing softly. She looks peaceful. I gently pick her up and carry her upstairs. Once I reach her room, I place her down on the bed, careful not to wake her. Her eyes pop open as I am pulling my arms out from underneath of her. My face is so close to hers, all I would have to do is lean in just a little and I could taste those sweet lips.

Hailey loops her arms around my neck. "Don't go," she whispers.

*Fuck!* I can't stay in here with her. What if Liam finds us? What if I'm unable to resist temptation, resist her?

"Just until I fall asleep," she mumbles. "Please."

"Anything you want, angel." Like I said, I can't tell her no.

She moves over to allow me space to join her. I climb in next to her, and she immediately attaches herself to my side and rests her head on my chest. My chest is rising rapidly as I struggle to pull deep even breaths into my lungs. After several minutes, she is still and I assume she has fallen asleep. I'm not ready to leave her, leave this moment with her. I gently stroke her hair and drop a kiss to her forehead.

I lie there holding her, lost in thought, trying to decipher these feelings and what I'm going to do about them. I glance over at the clock and realize it's four a.m. I have been holding her for three hours! As gently as I can, I remove my arm from underneath of her and get out of bed. I pull the covers up over her and drop a kiss to her forehead. "Sleep tight, angel," I whisper.

"I love you, Aiden," she says softly. So softly I almost don't hear her. I stop dead still, waiting for her to say more. Waiting for her to sit up, but she's still sleeping soundly. I drop to my knees beside the bed and gently brush the hair from her eyes. This girl, she wrecks me.

Those words, three little words, have brought me to my knees. I continue to watch her. I want to crawl back up in this bed and hold her tight. Fuck, I want to be inside of her. I just want her. I don't know how much longer I can fight this. I place a feather soft kiss on her lips and whisper, "I love you too, angel." And drag my tired ass to my room. I know she won't remember tonight. She won't remember that we both said "I love you" for the first time. I will though. I will never forget tonight as long as I live. I strip down to my boxer briefs and climb into bed. My bed and my arms feel empty. Life without Hailey would be empty.

# ~ 18 ~

## Hailey

I wake up with a pounding headache. I roll over to look at the clock, and see a bottle of water and two Advil sitting on the nightstand. At closer glance, I notice there is a note under the Advil.

Angel,

Take the Advil and drink the water. It will help,

I promise.

Aiden

I can't control the smile that breaks across my face. Aiden, for as much as he likes to pretend to be a hard ass, is really sweet. My mind wanders to what it would be like to be his. To have him be the one who is always there to pick me up or make sure I have a good hangover regimen. A soft knock at the door brings me back to the task at hand, Advil.

I hear the door open. I look up to find that Allison looks just like I feel. She slowly drags her feet until she reaches the bed. She climbs in next to me and burrows under the covers.

"My head hurts," she mumbles.

"Ditto," I say, trying to limit the conversation. My head is pounding, and the movement to drink the water and Advil did not help.

"The guys are making breakfast. Liam says we have to eat. It will help soak up the alcohol," she whispers.

"I don't think I can eat," I tell her.

"I know me either. That's what I told him, but he said it would make us feel better. I'm hiding out in here so maybe he won't make me."

I snort at that. Liam has never, and will never, make Allison do anything. He caters to her and will end up begging her to eat. He will so track her ass down. Hiding with me won't stop him, that's for sure.

"What's so funny?" Allison asks.

Before I can answer, my brother is at my door. "Hey, you two. You ready to eat something?"

Allie and I groan in unison and I hear Liam laugh. "I promise you will feel better after you eat. I didn't go crazy, just made pancakes and bacon. Come on, let's go."

"We don't want to," Allie whines.

"Baby, you have to. The food will help soak up all the alcohol," Liam tries to reason.

"It hurts to move," she mumbles.

"I can carry you, beautiful, but I really need you to eat," he says this as he leans down and scoops her up in his arms and heads for the kitchen.

Thinking I'm off the hook, I lay back down and throw the covers over my head. More sleep. I just need a few more hours and I will be good to go. I hear a low chuckle, and immediately I know it's Aiden. It's like my body can sense when he is near me.

He pulls the cover off my body. "Let's go, angel. We need to get some food in you," he tells me.

"No. Don't wanna move. Hurts to move," I mumble, while reaching for the blankets that he just stole.

"Sorry, no can do. You need to eat, and since Allison was unable to walk, I am here as your personal travel arrangements," he says, pulling the covers out of my hands. My brain is still slow to register in my post alcohol state. Which is why when he leans down and scoops me up in his arms, I'm unable to protest. Well, that and it feels nice. Almost like I was here just recently.

"This feels like Deja vu," I say out loud.

Aiden laughs softly before placing his lips next to my ear. "That's because I had you in my arms last night, angel," he whispers.

I stiffen at his words. Holy shit, did something happen between us? Shit. Shit. Shit.

As if he can read my mind, he says, "Relax, crazy girl. I carried you to bed last night and tucked you in. Nothing happened." He drops a kiss on my temple just as we round the corner into the kitchen.

"Here is our other underage alcoholic," he teases as he gently places me in a chair that Liam pulls out for me. Aiden proceeds to pour me a glass of orange juice and a cup of coffee. Once he sets them in front of me, he places two pancakes and a couple of pieces of bacon on my plate. Finally, he takes the seat beside me and begins making his own plate.

I chance a subtle look at Liam and Allie to see if they notice all the attention that Aiden is giving me. They don't. I stare down at my plate, trying to wrap my head around all the emotions that are bouncing around. I want Aiden, and he is giving me all these mixed signals. GAH! I just need to ignore what my heart is trying to say, and focus on what I know is right. Aiden is just being nice, a good friend. That's all.

Aiden leans in close to me. "Did you take your Advil, angel?" he whispers.

Nodding my head, that is still pounding. "Yes, thank you," I reply quietly.

Aiden nods and goes right back to eating. I pick up my fork and begin to eat. Chewing hurts my head. Hell, who am I kidding? Breathing hurts my head. How anyone can do this, drink themselves silly on a regular basis, is beyond me. It'll be a while before I indulge again. I hate feeling like ass.

The guys send us off to lounge while they clean the kitchen. I can definitely get used to this treatment. It's usually Allie and I cooking for them. They always help clean up, but it's a rare occasion that they do both. *Ah, the joys in life.*

Allison decides she wants to take a nap, so she and Liam go to their room. I am too comfortable to move. I am curled up on the couch. It's a rainy day, so there is not much else to do. Once I'm awake, it's hard for me to go back to sleep no matter how tired I am. I'm weird like that.

Aiden comes into the living room and I automatically lift my legs, inviting him to sit with me on the couch. I keep reminding myself that we are friends and we have done this exact thing a thousand times. He takes a seat on the opposite end of the couch and I rest my legs on his lap.

"We watching a movie?" he asks me.

"Yeah, but you can pick," I tell him, tossing him the remote. Aiden grins and starts flipping through the channels. My head is turned towards the television, but my eyes are trained on Aiden. He is gorgeous. His brown hair is messy. I can tell he just ran his fingers through it after his shower this morning. I love his thick locks. My fingers itch to touch him. To run my fingers through his hair.

Aiden settles on the Lifetime Movie Network. I smile. He knows me so well.

"For me?" I ask and bat my eyelashes.

Aiden just smiles and winks. He picks up my left foot and begins to massage it. This is new; he's never done this before. Friends can give friends a foot massage, right?

I lie there with his hands on my feet, working their magic. I'm trying to concentrate on the movie, but I can't. I close my eyes to try to calm my racing heart. I focus on taking in deep even breaths. I feel my body relax and I start to drift off to sleep.

I slowly wake up and open my eyes. I see that the television is muted and the house is quiet. I lift my head and I see that Aiden is still at his end of the couch. He's awake and he's watching me.

"Hey. Sorry I fell asleep on you," I say my voice raspy. I could really use something to drink.

As if he can read my mind, Aiden leans over, plucks a bottle of water from the coffee table, and hands it to me.

"Thanks," I say, taking it from him and chugging half of it. Much better.

"How was the movie?" I ask, my voice now back to normal.

Aiden shrugs his shoulders. "I'm not sure, I didn't finish it," he says.

"I glance at the television and see that it is, indeed, still on." I look back at Aiden and raise my eyebrows in question.

"You looked so peaceful, I didn't want it to wake you up." He shrugs. "I know you didn't get a lot of sleep last night and needed to rest."

"So…uh…what did you do?" I ask. I'm not sure how to take his last statement. Do friends just do that? Do they go out of their way to make sure the other gets rested after a drunken night? He's in the same spot as when I fell asleep. Did he…did he watch me?

Aiden's face flushes slightly. "I watched you," he says softly.

*He watched me!* I open my mouth to respond, and no words will come out. I'm stunned speechless. I open and close my mouth again, still nothing. I know I look like a damn fish right now, which is totally embarrassing, but… Holy Shit! Aiden watched me sleep for, what, like an hour?

"You could have moved. I probably wouldn't have woken up," I tell him.

"Yeah, that really wasn't an option for me. Why would I want to move, when I can be close to my angel when she's sleeping?" he asks.

*Fuck me!* He is totally being serious right now, and talk about fucking swooooon! He has no idea what he's doing to me. His words affect me like nothing else ever has. He affects me like nothing or no one else. How much longer can I hide my feelings for him? Better question, what the hell is going on with him? Friends don't say those kind of things to friends. The lines are blurring more and more every day, and I don't know which way is up. I feel like I'm drowning in the sea of Aiden Emerson. The only problem is, I can't decide if I want to sink or swim.

I realize I have lost myself to my internal freak out and that Aiden is still watching me. I need to say something, but what the fuck kind of response do I give to that? I take a deep breath and go with all that I can say, without telling him I am madly in love with him and have been for a while now. I dig deep and pull out my southern hospitality.

"Thank you," I say barely above a whisper.

Aiden squeezes my leg in reply just as Liam and Allison walk into the room. Liam plops down in the recliner and pulls Allison down on top of him.

"The weather is shit today, man," Liam says to Aiden. "We only have a few days left. I hope it clears up before we have to leave."

"I don't see that happening. I watched the weather earlier, and they are calling for rain the next three days," he says solemnly.

My mouth is moving and words are spewing out before I can comprehend what I'm saying. "Maybe we should just pack up and head home. You three have to pack and sign the lease for your new condo, anyway," I remind him.

Aiden's grip on my leg tightens and I can see his jaw clench. Did he change his mind about living with Liam and Allie?

"Probably not a bad idea. We can't enjoy the beach with it pouring down rain," Allison says.

"Well it's two o'clock now, do we pack up and head out today, or leave first thing in the morning?" Liam asks.

"We're getting low on supplies, so maybe we should just go now," Allie says to him.

"All right, beautiful, let's get packed. What do you say we leave here around four? Will that give you guys enough time to get packed?"

"Sure," I say, and Aiden just nods his head.

I lift my legs off his lap and jump up off the couch. I head to my room to pack and get a little distance. Distance from the man who holds my heart in his hands and has no idea.

# ~ 19 ~

# *Aiden*

What the fuck! We're leaving three days early. Three days! I'm not ready to let her go yet. Once we get back to Chapel Hill, we will be packing up and moving to Charlotte. And Hales, she'll still be in Chapel Hill. Three hours away. I realize, in the grand scheme of things, three hours is nothing. However, Hales has school and once training camp starts, my life will be live, eat, and breathe football. I knew leaving her behind would be hard. What I didn't count on was feeling like my heart was being ripped out of my chest.

I stomp up stairs to my room and begin throwing my things in my bags, slamming drawers as I go. I can't help but feel like I'm being cheated. This was my time with her before we had to leave. Time to work through these feelings and come to a decision. The only decision that was made is that I'm in love with her. I'm packing my fucking bags to go home and move three hours away from the only girl I have ever loved. I don't think anyone will ever compare to Hailey.

Apparently, through all the banging drawers, I didn't hear Allie come into my room. She is sitting on the chair in the corner, just watching me.

"What?" I snap at her. My anger has nothing to do with her, but she's here.

"You want to talk about it?" she asks, not a bit fazed by my foul mood.

"Nothing to talk about," I snap yet again.

Allison smiles. "Ace, you're my family. I know when something's wrong."

"It's nothing, all right," I say in a much more clam voice, at least, I try to.

"How about I give it a shot?" she asks.

She stands up, walks to the bed, and sits down. She pats the spot next to her. I sigh and sit down beside her. I bend over and rest my elbows on my knees while running my fingers through my hair. I'm on the verge of losing my shit. I mean literally breaking down. I'm fighting like hell to not let my feelings show.

"This is how I see it," Allison begins. "You're in love with Hailey. You're pissed off because we're leaving early, which means you're losing time with her." She places her hand on my back and begins to rub soothing circles. I don't move my position. I am barely holding my shit together.

"You're pissed off because you thought you could work her out of your system. Spend a little time with her, realize the feelings were minor at best, and you could move to Charlotte without another thought except for how your friend is doing. You're scared because if your relationship with Hailey becomes more, what happens if it falls apart? You lose her. She will no longer be a part of your life. Or can she? Will you both be able to move past whatever issues caused the break up and still be friends?"

Fuck me! Ash just hit the nail on the head. "How do you...?"

"I told you, we're family. I know you better than anyone, and I can read you. I also went through the same situation of wanting someone I thought I could never have. I wanted Liam from the moment I met him, but I was too afraid that I'd be just another notch on the bed post for him. Look how things turned out for us," she says with a smile.

I lift my head and face Allison. "It's too risky," I croak out, my voice thick with emotion. "I can't imagine my life without her in it. If I pursue her and things don't work out, I lose her all together. I can't handle that. I know I can't. I…" I swallow and take a deep breath. "I just won't risk it, okay?"

"I get it. I do. Just think about this. Think about you and Hales being together and having what Liam and I have? Think about how it would be if things did work out." She stands and places a kiss on my cheek; then turns and leaves the room.

I lie back on the bed and stare at the ceiling. Allison's words are running through my mind. What would it be like for Hales and I to have what they have? To be able to hold her and kiss her anytime I wanted. To know that she is mine, and when dumb fucks like Seth try to hit on her, it wouldn't just be pretending to be the jealous boyfriend. Well, pretending to be the boyfriend. The jealously is alive and well. I could have ripped his fucking head off the day I saw him put his arm around her. I want that, I do. I want everything with her. I want us to be more, but I am too afraid. Shit, being around Liam has turned me into a pussy.

Pulling myself off the bed, I resume packing, this time I'm quieter. Instead of the anger that was consuming me before, now it's just sadness and pain. The painful ache in my chest is still there. I need to put on my big boy panties and fucking deal with the decision that I've made. I'm the one choosing not to risk losing her to try for more. I'm the one who has to suck it up and deal.

A slight knock on my door catches my attention. I glance up, but no one enters. "Come in," I yell.

Hailey slowly pushes the door open. "Hey, you all packed?" she asks.

"Almost, how about you?" I reply.

"Yeah, I just threw it all in my bags. I can sort it out later. I just wanted to come and talk to you for a few minutes. I know when we get home things are going to be hectic."

She's chewing on her bottom lip, so I know she's nervous. "What's up?" I ask, concerned.

She shrugs her shoulders. "I just needed a minute with you."

Hailey! God, I want to wrap my arms around her and tell her we're okay. That it's all going to work out. I know I can't do that.

I've made my decision and I need to stand by it. I decide playful Aiden is the best approach.

I reach up and tap her nose with my index finger "Aw, are you gonna miss me?" I tease.

Her eyes find mine and what I see is sadness. I can't look away from her. "More than you know," she whispers.

Wrecked! I am completely fucking wrecked by this girl. All thoughts of keeping my distance fly out the window. She's hurting and I need to comfort her. I reach out and pull her against my chest. I feel her tremble as she softly cries into my shirt.

"Angel, I will only be three hours away. If you need me, I can get to you before you even realize I'm gone. I promise we will still see each other. Not every day, but we will. I will make it happen," I say gently, rubbing my hand up and down her back, trying like hell to comfort her.

"You guys are moving on without me," she whimpers. "You'll have new exciting lives. You'll forget about me."

I lean back and gently place my fingers under her chin and lift her head so we are eye to eye. "Angel, I need you to listen to me and listen good, okay?" I ask her. She nods her head slightly.

"Baby, you are not forgettable. No matter how far away from you I am, you will always be here." I place her hand over my heart. "And here." I take her other hand and point to my head. She gently runs her fingers through my hair. "You will always be important to me. I won't be able to see you every day, but I need you to understand that I would do anything for you. Do you understand?" I plead with her.

I rest my forehead against hers. "You are so special to me. I need you to always remember that. If you need me, no matter what it is, I'm yours," I tell her. I mean that. She owns me like no one else ever will.

"Okay," she whispers.

Liam yells out in the hallway as he passes, "Emerson, you ready to roll, man?"

"I'll be out in a minute," I yell back.

"I'll let you get back to packing." She pulls away and turns to leave, but stops when she reaches the door. "Thank you," she says softly.

"Angel, please remember what I said," I plead with her. I need to know that she understands that there is nothing I wouldn't do for her.

Hailey nods her head and leaves the room.

I bend over and place my hands on my knees, breathing deep, dragging breath into my lungs. *Shit!* I want her so fucking bad. It kills me to see her hurting like this. If Liam wouldn't have interrupted us, I don't know what I would have done. My control is slipping and my chest is filled with a deep ache that only Hailey can heal. This shit is so fucking hard. Wanting to make her mine and not allowing myself to do so…Is. So. Fucking. Hard. How in the hell am I going to be able to do this?

# ~ 20 ~

# Hailey

I flee from Aiden's room and rush into mine. As soon as I close the door, hot tears rush from my eyes. My heart is broken. Aiden is so good to me and so sweet. He has no idea that his words crush me. He's amazing and his offer to always be there for me is amazing, but I want him to be mine. If he knew that, he would not have said any of that. He would be running for the hills. I can't believe I actually told him that I needed a minute with him. What. The. Hell.

I'm sure he thinks I'm a fucking nut job about now. I guess it's better than the embarrassment of knowing that his best friend's little sister is madly in love with him. Hell, if he knew that, he would head straight to Charlotte from here and never look back.

I go to the bathroom and wash my face, trying to wash away my tears. I finish packing and drag my bags to the living room. Allison comes rushing to me.

"Hales, what's wrong?" she asks, concerned.

"I'm just going to miss you guys so much," I say as the tears begin to fall yet again. At least Aiden won't know that most of them are for him. For the love I have for him that he will never know about.

"Come here, you," Liam says, walking over and pulling me into his arms.

"You, my baby sister, are not even going to notice that we're gone. You can come up on weekends and we'll come visit as well." He hugs me tight.

111

"I can come down and stay with you while the guys are busy with training camp," Allie offers. I hear Liam groan. The big lug hates being away from her.

"I'm okay," I say, stepping away from Liam. "I just let my emotions get the best of me." I offer them a sad smile.

"Let's go, my bestie. You and I are riding in the back. We need some girl time," Allison says, pulling me outside.

Liam and Aiden load our bags and lock up the beach house before piling in the Pathfinder, and we hit the road. The road to home, and for me, the road to loneliness.

The ride home is filled with Allison and I making plans for how we're going to keep in touch. We make plans for me to come up and stay the week with them before school starts. The three of them continue to talk about how I won't even notice their gone. *Yeah right!*

The next week is a whirlwind of activity. Liam, Allison, and Aiden drive to Charlotte and look at the condos their agent has found for them. Instead of staying alone, I drive to my parents to spend some time there. I was invited to go along, but decided that I needed to start this now. Next week they will be gone. Living three hours away. I need to start dealing with how I'm going to muddle through without them.

I really want to talk to my parents anyway. I need to tell them that I want to transfer schools. I was accepted to Durham Tech College in the Associates of Nursing Program. I want to be a Registered Nurse. The program is two years, but I have all of my pre-requisites out of the way. All I have to do is pass a nursing assistant course prior to classes starting in September. I can be finished with college in a year! I have the registration paperwork in my purse and the course starts next week. I have always loved helping people, and have been thinking about this for a while now. I was so excited when I got in, but I didn't tell anyone. I'm not sure why I didn't tell them. I guess I want to make sure mom and dad are on board before I announce anything. Besides, the three of them have their hands full with moving, and then the guys start training camp next week. I'll tell them once things settle down.

I pull into my parents' driveway and they are sitting on the front porch swing. Mom is reading her kindle and dad is reading the newspaper. I can feel the grin that takes over my face. My parents have an amazing marriage. I can only hope that I find that. The forever kind of love.

"Well, who do we owe for this nice surprise?" my dad says as I climb the steps to the front porch.

"Hey, you two," I say, skipping over and kissing dad on the cheek and giving mom a hug.

"It's nice to see you," my mom tells me.

"Well, I missed you guys and I kind of have something to talk to you about," I say shyly. Why? I have no clue. My parents have always been supportive of me. I guess I'm afraid they will be disappointed that I want to transfer from UNC.

"Pull up a chair, sweetheart, we're all ears," My dad says, laying his newspaper on the table next to him. My mom hands him her kindle and I have their full attention. I'm not surprised at this. Anytime Liam and I want to talk, they are always there to listen.

I sit down on the wooden lounge chair that my dad and Liam built one summer. Mom said they were "bonding" before Liam went off to college. I smile at the memory.

"Well, I kind of wanted to talk to you about school. I finally declared a major," I say.

"Hailey, that's terrific. So what did you choose?" mom asks.

"Well, you see, that's what I wanted to talk to you about. I'm going to have to transfer schools." I stop to gage their reaction. They are both still looking at me, smiling. I take that as a good sign and continue. "I was accepted to the RN program at Durham Tech. I want to be a nurse. I have all of my pre-requisites completed and now just need to focus on the nursing portion. I can be done in a year. I already moved out of the dorms and into the condo, so that won't be an issue. And I called the school and I have until August to withdraw and get a full refund for my tuition." I rush to get it all in. I'm nervous of their reaction and excited all at the same time. I really want to do this.

"Hailey, I'm so proud of you," my dad tells me.

"What can we do to help?" My mom asks, and just like that, I expel the breath that I was holding. My parents truly are amazing.

I jump out of my chair and rush to the swing. I bend down and hug them both. Tears running down my face. "Thank you so much!" I say through my tears. "I really want this. I want to be a nurse and to have your support. I love you guys," I say.

Dad chuckles. "We love you too, my sweet girl. Now tell us more about this new career of yours."

We spend the next hour talking on the front porch about nursing and the assistant class that I start next week. Mom tells me to let her know if she can do anything, and to try not to get overwhelmed. She even tries to get me to move home so she can take care of things like my laundry, so all I have to focus on is school. How I won the parent lottery, I have no idea, but I am so thankful for them.

I eat dinner with my parents and then head back to the condo. It's quiet. Too quiet, but this is something I'm going to have to get used to. I curl up on the couch with my kindle and the remote. I don't want to watch television, but I need the noise to drown out the quiet. I miss them.

Just as I am about to pick my new book boyfriend for the evening, my cell phone rings. It's Allison. "Hey, you," I say in greeting.

"Hey, yourself. What are you up to?" she asks.

"Not much. Had dinner with mom and dad and just got home. I was getting ready to pick my man of the evening," I tell her.

"Ooh, I'm so jealous. We have looked at condos all day, but we finally found one. It's amazing, and you will have your own room when you come to stay with us," she says happily.

I smile. "That's awesome, I hope you took pictures."

"Yes, and you're still coming to spend a week before school starts right?" she inquires.

I mentally go over the nursing assistant class and the start date at Durham Tech. I will have one week between the two. "Yep, that's the plan," I reply. "So what are you all up to now?" I ask her.

"Well, we are stopping to get something to eat, and then we are headed home."

"Home? I thought you were staying the night?" I ask.

"Well, we were, but it's only six o'clock. We should be home around nine. We all decided we just wanted to come home. We have a lot of packing and things to do."

"Okay, well I guess I'll see you guys in a little while. Drive safe," I tell her.

"We will. Liam drove down, so Aiden is driving back. I missed having you with us," she says quietly.

"Me too, but this is the new us. We are going to have to learn to adjust," I say.

"Yeah, but that doesn't mean I have to like it. See you soon," she says as she ends the call.

I'm shocked that their coming home, but then again, they do have to pack up their lives and move. These next few days are going to take a toll on me emotionally.

I wake to the sound of keys in the door. I open my eyes and see Liam, Aiden, and Allison dragging in their overnight bags. I sit up and rub my eyes. My kindle falls to the floor. "Shit!" I say.

"Well, that's a welcome greeting." Liam laughs.

"Shut it, buster. I just dropped my kindle and that, my dear brother, is a tragedy," I retort.

"Shit, it didn't break, did it?" Allison asks concerned. *I love my best friend!*

"Nope, all is well," I say. "How was the drive home?"

"Long," Allison says. "But worth it. I want to show you the condo." She pulls out her phone and proceeds to show me each room.

"Wow, it looks great. You took a ton of pictures." I laugh at her.

"I wanted you to see everything, that way you can be a part of this with us."

I reach my arm around her and hug her tight. "Thank you," I say, my voice thick with emotion.

"Hey, what's this?" Aiden asks. He's holding my admission letter from Durham Tech.

Here we go. "That's my acceptance letter to the RN program at Durham Tech," I say, like that letter doesn't change the course of my life.

"What? You're changing schools?" Liam asks.

"Yeah, I am. I talked to mom and dad about it tonight." I proceed to tell them about the program, how I have everything I need, and will just have to focus on nursing classes. I tell them about the nursing assistant class and how it will run up until the week that I come to stay with them in Charlotte.

"You're still coming though, right?" Aiden asks me.

"Of course. I get a week off before the heavy stuff starts, and I can't think of a better way to spend it than hanging with my family," I tell him.

I see his jaw clinch at me including him in the "family" category. I need to think of him as a brother; otherwise, all I think about is ripping his damn clothes off.

# ~ 21 ~

# *Aiden*

We finally chose a condo, and it's so sweet! We decide to drive home instead of spending the night. It was Liam's idea. He said we could get an early start on packing tomorrow. I don't really care what his reasoning is if it gets me back to Hales that much faster. I missed her today. It's usually the four of us and, well, I just really missed her. Moving without her is going to suck. I wonder if I can convince her to transfer schools so she can live with us in Charlotte.

"Dude, where's the fire?" Liam asks me from the backseat.

I glance at the dash and realize I'm driving eighty miles an hour. I smile. Just thinking about Hales makes me drive faster. I really missed her today. *Get used to it, Emerson.*

"Sorry, just anxious to be home. It's been a long day." A long day without Hailey.

We finally arrive, and the three of us grab our bags and head inside. Hailey jumps up from the couch when she hears us. I try to hide my smile, but I'm too damn happy to see her. We talk about the condo and the fact that she will have her own room. I wish she would call my room hers. I see a paper lying on the floor, so I bend down to pick it up. "What's this?" I ask her.

The smile falls from her face, which puts me on alert. Hailey then begins telling us how she's changing schools and has decided she wants to be a nurse. My chest swells with pride for her. She's amazing, and her choosing to be a nurse just flows with the type of person she is. I'm dragged back to the conversation when I hear her tell us that she only has a week between some summer course she has to take and classes starting. I feel the panic build; I'm counting on seeing her that week.

"You're still coming though, right?" I ask her hopefully.

When she agrees that yes, she will still be spending the week with us, I relax until she says that she wants nothing more than to hang out with her family that week.

What. The. Fuck.

Yes, I think of her as family. In my mind, she's mine. Not just my family, but my girl. To hear her lumping me into the "family" category pisses me the fuck off. I know she isn't considering me the same type of family that I consider her. I have no right to be pissed about it, but fuck it, I am.

"Good," I say, handing the letter to her. "Well, I'm beat. See you all tomorrow." I turn and head to my room. I wanted to spend time with her tonight, but damn it, I need to get my shit under control. I can't be getting pissed off because of these feelings I have for her.

It's not her fault that I fell in love with her.

I take a hot shower and wash the day away. Hoping I can relax, I climb into bed and reach for the remote. I scroll through our five hundred channels and nothing catches my eye. No wonder. The only thing that tends to be catching my eye lately is sleeping in my living room. I turn the TV off and I'm engulfed in darkness. I stare at the ceiling, listening to the quiet of the house. I heard Liam and Allison go to bed a while ago.

I want to see her. I know she'll be sleeping, but I just need to see her before I can fall asleep. I throw the covers back and climb out of bed. I softly open my door and make my way down the hall. When I make it to the living room, I find Hailey curled up in a ball on the couch. Her soft pink lips are parted and she's softly breathing in and out. She looks so peaceful. So beautiful. I lean down and brush her hair out of her eyes. She doesn't stir. I bend down and kiss her forehead. "Sweet dreams, angel." I say, and then head back to my room. I don't want to. I want to pick her up and bring her with me. Hold her in my arms, but I can't and I won't. I just needed to see her. Just two more days and I won't have that option anymore. And there it is, that familiar ache that is taking over my chest these days.

I climb back into bed and stare into the darkness. I fall asleep with the image of Hailey curled up on the couch running through my mind.

The next day is nothing short of chaos. Liam, Allison, and I pack up our lives. This is all surreal to me. Liam and I made it to the NFL. My best friends are getting married, and the girl of my dreams is being left behind.

"You all set?" I hear from the doorway. I look up and find Hailey watching me.

"Yeah, pretty much. I just have the clothes I have on, my stuff for tomorrow, and the essentials left to pack," I reply.

"Yeah, Liam and Allie are pretty much ready as well. They're taking a nap."

She looks amazing today. She has on short gym shorts and a UNC t-shirt. Her hair is pulled up in some kind of knot on top of her head. She has not one stick of make-up on, and she has never looked better.

"I'm getting kind of hungry. You want to go grab something to eat?" I ask her.

"Sure." She looks down at herself. "Can we maybe hit a drive through?" she asks with a grimace.

If she only knew how she looked to me, right now, in this moment. She's fucking hot!

"Anything you want, angel. For the record, you look amazing as always," I tell her honestly.

She rolls those sexy blue eyes at me and walks away. What do I do? I watch her of course. Her ass looks amazing in those shorts.

I grab my wallet and cell phone and meet her by the front door. "I drive, you buy," she says, holding up her keys.

I nod my head in agreement and we head out. "You choose. You know I can eat anything," I tell her.

The car ride is silent, yet comfortable. I'm enjoying just spending time with her.

Hailey pulls into Chipotle, turns to me and smiles.

"Since when did Chipotle get a drive through?" I ask her.

Smiling sweetly, she says, "I was hoping you wouldn't mind going in and ordering. Then we can go to the park to eat."

"I said anything you want," I tell her, opening the car door. Like I could tell her no anyway.

"Wait, you don't even know what I want," she tells me.

I smile at that, because I do know. She always gets the same thing. "Burrito Bowl, brown rice, chicken, hot salsa, sour cream, lettuce, cheese, chips, and a large lemonade," I tell her through the window.

Her mouth drops open.

"Did you want to add anything?" I ask her.

She shakes her head no, and I walk away with a smile on my face. She has no idea that I watch every move she makes, I memorize what she likes and dislikes. The look on her face was priceless. *Score!*

There is no one in line, which surprises me. This place is usually packed. I order our food, fill our drinks at the drink counter, and head back to the car.

I stop at the driver's side window and Hailey takes our drinks from my hands. I then head to the passenger side and get it. "Driver, to the park, please," I say, teasing her.

She just laughs and pulls out. It only takes about five minutes to make it to the park. We pull into the lot and there are no other cars. We gather our lunch and head to a picnic table that is nestled at the edge of a tree line. It's the most secluded spot in the park and it's usually taken. I can't help but think that everything is falling into place to make this a perfect day with her. No line at the restaurant, the park is deserted, Liam and Allie wanted alone time, so it's just us. Me and my girl.

"So, tell me about school," I say, opening her bowl for her and handing her a fork.

In reward, I get one of her dazzling smiles. "I'm really excited," she says softly.

"I'm so proud of you Hales. You are going to be an amazing nurse," I say, digging into my bowl.

"It's going to be hard work and a lot of dedication, but with you all leaving…well, I'll have plenty of time to focus on studying," she replies, staring down at her food.

"Hey." I reach over and lift her chin with my forefinger so her eyes meet mine. "We're not leaving you. I am not leaving you. You will always be a part of us. Once you finish school, you can move to Charlotte and live with us. We made sure that you have your own room. It's just a year," I tell her. She is staring at me; the expression on her face gives nothing away about how she's feeling. "It's as if you applying and getting accepted into the program is a sign. You will be with us in a year; otherwise, you would have been at UNC for three more years. One year, angel, and we will all be together again."

The ache in my chest eases a little just thinking that a year from now, she will be living with us again, and all will be right in the world.

"I guess you're right. So, are you excited about training camp?" she asks.

The rest of the afternoon, we sit there at the picnic table and talk about, well, everything. I'm gonna fucking miss this girl so much.

My cell phone rings, making us both jump. Hailey giggles as I pull it out of my pocket and swipe the screen. It's Liam.

"Hey, man," I say, smiling at Hailey as she continues to giggle.

"Dude, where the fuck are you, and have you seen Hales?" he says curtly.

I laugh, "I'm looking right at her."

"Where in the hell are you guys?"

"We were hungry, so we went to Chipotle and brought it to the park," I tell him.

"Fuck me. That sounds so good right now. When are you guys coming back?"

"Hales, are you about ready to go," I reluctantly ask her. Not ready for our time together to end.

"Yeah, I guess we better. It's getting late."

"We're heading back now," I tell Liam.

"Cool, hey, do you mind stopping to pick up Chipotle for Allie and me? She said she would call the order in so you don't have to wait."

"Yeah, we can do that," I tell him.

# ~ 22 ~

# *Hailey*

Yesterday was one of the hardest days of my life. I said a very tearful goodbye to my three best friends. Yes, I include my brother in that title because, well, Liam is the best brother ever! He also gets major brownie points for making Allie my sister.

Allie and I made plans for me to visit a month from now, the last week of August. My nursing assistant classes end the week before and Nursing school starts the week after. I doubt I will make it down before that, even for just a day or weekend trip. I really need to focus on this class or I can't start nursing classes. The three of them will be busy getting settled into their new place, so I doubt they will visit either. So there it is. An entire month before I see my three favorite people again.

Today is my first day of nursing assisting class. The program consists of two weeks of class work and two weeks of an externship. At the end of the extern, I take a final exam to pass my certification. It's either pass or fail. Lucky for me, I have no distractions, nothing but time to focus on passing.

I walk into class and take a seat near the back; I am the first one to arrive. My nursing advisor already told me that the class is small, only twelve students. They only take a few select students into the nursing program each year, so they get more individualized attention from the instructors. Our nursing class has twenty-six students; the others have already completed this course.

I'm barely seated when a girl my age strolls in and sits down beside me. I look over and smile at her.

"Hey! I'm Macie," she says, thrusting her hand out for me to shake.

"Nice to meet you, I'm Hailey," I say.

"So are you nervous about this?" she questions.

"Yes, you?" I reply.

"Holy shit! You have no idea. I've worried myself to death. I have busted my ass to get into this program on scholarship and this is my last piece of the puzzle. If I screw this up, I'm out," she says in a rush.

"Well, what do you say we partner up, study together?" I ask. I'm not sure where the invitation came from, but I can tell already that Macie is nice, and having a study partner would be beneficial. Besides, it's not like I have anyone waiting on me at home.

"Really? That would be awesome. We are so going to nail this," she says with confidence.

Wow, she is a lot like me. "So are you from around here?" I ask.

"Yep, born and raised. You?"

"I live in Chapel Hill, so basically yes. I'm a UNC transfer. I really want to be a nurse. They offer a Bachelor's program but I want it now. I'm an instant gratification kinda girl." I laugh.

"You and me both. My mom and dad work hard, but still couldn't afford to send both my brother and I to college. We are both here on scholarships. I don't know if it's a twin thing or what, but we both wanted to get a two year degree so we could get out into the work force. Take some of the burden off our parents, you know?" she tells me.

"Wow, you're a twin?" I ask.

"Seriously, that's all you got out of the conversation?"

"I...I...Um..."

"Relax, I'm just kidding. Yes, I'm a twin. My brother Miles is a student here also. He's a computer programming major," she chirps. "Any siblings?"

I hesitate. Do I tell her about Liam and the NFL? I decide to wait a while before I divulge that piece of information. "Yeah, I have a brother, Liam. He just graduated from UNC and moved to Charlotte with my best friend, who also happens to be his fiancée, and his best friend Aiden." There, that's all true I just didn't mention that both Liam and Aiden just got drafted to the Panthers.

"Cool." Is all she can reply before the instructor of the class clears her throat and begins going over the syllabus.

Class is long, five hours each day for two weeks. My head is spinning from all of the information that she just gave us. I got this, at least I keep telling myself that.

"So, Hailey, do you have any plans for tonight?" Macie asks me.

"Uh, no, not really. Why?" I ask her.

"My brother and I are having a small get together at the house tonight. My dad's an over the road truck driver and he had to go to Charleston. My mom went with him so she could visit with my Aunt Sarah who lives there. Miles and I have the house to ourselves," she says.

"Yeah, okay. What time should I be there?"

"Come at six, that way I can introduce you to everyone as they show up."

"Sounds good. Thanks, Macie."

She hands me her phone. "Add your number and I'll text you the address."

I quickly program my number and hand it back to her. Her thumbs fly across the keyboard as she sends me the address. Two second later, my phone pings with a message. I add Macie to my contacts list.

"Well, I guess I'll see you in a few hours," I say.

"Sounds great, see you then. Call if you get lost or anything," she calls over her shoulder.

When I get home, the emptiness of the condo surrounds me once again. It's really going to take some time to get used to this. I make my way down the hall towards my bedroom. Now that Liam and Aiden have moved out, I have an actual room. I chose Aiden's room to be mine. I just want to feel closer to him. I know it's a bit stalkerish, but I still couldn't resist.

I stand in front of my closet and begin to tear through the hangers looking for something to wear tonight. I decide on short blue jean shorts, light and dark pink layer tanks, and my pink flip flops. Casual. Macie said it was just a few friends, and I don't want it to seem like I'm trying too hard to impress them.

I hop in the shower and rinse off the day, not washing my hair. I decide to leave it down tonight. I dress quickly in my outfit, slip into my flip flops, add some lip gloss and mascara, and I'm good to go.

I find Macie's house with no trouble. Pulling into the driveway, I'm suddenly nervous. I decide someone needs to know where I am, so I call the main number to the condo.

Allison picks up on the first ring. "Hello?"

"Hey!" I say, excited to hear her voice. It's only been a couple days since they left, but God, I miss them.

"Hales, how are you? How was class today?" she asks, genuinely interested in how it went.

I spend a few minutes discussing the class and how excited I am for everything to start. Allie tells me that they are settling in and are almost unpacked.

"Listen, I don't have a lot of time to talk, but I met a girl in class today that invited me to her house tonight for what she referred to as a small get together. I just pulled into the drive, but I wanted to let someone know where I was, you know, just in case," I tell her.

"I'm glad to hear you're going out. Can you just text me the address and make sure you call me as soon as you get home," she says sternly.

I laugh. "Yes, mother. Anyway, I need to go. I'll call you tomorrow and we can catch up."

"Sounds good. Be safe," she tells me.

I shove my phone in my pocket, along with my keys, and lock my car. I walk up to the front door and ring the bell. I take a deep breath to try and calm my nerves.

I'm startled when the door flies open and I am met with a muscular, tattooed, shirtless chest. My eyes move up and meet dark chocolate ones. "Hey, beautiful. What can I do for ya?" the sexy stranger asks me.

Before I get a chance to speak, Macie appears behind him, smacking his shoulder. "This is the girl I was telling you about that I met in class today. She's off limits to you," she tells him.

I stand there starting at the two of them and I can now see the resemblance. They both have sandy blonde hair and dark chocolate eyes. This must be Miles.

"Hailey, this is my brother, Miles. Miles, this is Hailey," she introduces us.

"Nice to meet you," I say.

"The pleasure is all mine, sweetheart," Miles says, grinning.

I can't help but blush at his attention. I've spent so much time with Aiden and Liam, that getting hit on is rare for me. Even if the guy tries, they have him scared off in no time. Not anymore. It's just me. I'm not sure how I feel about that.

"Right. Okay, well, I'm just setting up in the kitchen, care to help?" Macie asks.

"Sure, lead the way," I tell her in a voice that sounds way more confident than what I really am.

"Just ignore my idiot brother. He's a total flirt," Macie says, handing me a jar of salsa and a bowl. I don't reply, because really, what do I say? I'm flattered that your twin brother was flirting with me? I don't have a lot of experience with it because my older brother and his best friend, who by the way I'm in love with, scare guys away before we even get that far? Yeah, I'll just kept quiet on this one.

127

By the time Macie and I are finished with the snacks, the house is starting to fill. There are at least thirty people here. Macie pulls me to the living room and starts introducing me to people; her best friend Holly is one of them. I hope she doesn't expect me to remember all these names.

Macie excuses herself to go to the restroom, and I find myself standing alone in the living room. I lean against the wall and pull out my phone. I'm scrolling through Facebook when a shadow falls over me. I raise my head and see Miles, in all of his bad boy sexiness, standing over me.

"Hey, sweetheart, why are you all alone?" he asks me.

"Macie just went to the restroom and I really don't know anyone else," I tell him honestly.

"Come with me," he says, placing his tattooed arm around my shoulders and guiding me to the other side of the room.

"Well, well, well, what do we have here?" A tall guy with more tattoos than Miles asks with a friendly smile.

"This is Hailey. Hailey this is my best friend Kaden," Miles introduces us.

"It's nice to meet you," I say to Kaden.

"You too," Kaden says with a wink. He, too, is all kinds of sexy.

The music changes to Aerosmith's "Walk This Way" and I can't help but sway to the beat. *This song rocks!*

Miles smiles at me as he hands his beer to Kaden and pulls me onto the makeshift dance floor. We begin to dance separately at first, but as we get into it, we move closer together. I turn and my back is against his chest. He places his hands on my hips and I bring my arms up over my head and drape them behind me around his neck. Miles pulls me closer and I grind into him. By the time the song is over, we are facing each other, his hands still on my hips, my hands still around his neck, his leg between mine, and we are grinding. He's smiling and laughing, and so am I.

The song ends and we walk back to Kaden. "Holy fucking shit! That was fucking hot! Please tell me I'm next," he begs.

Miles and I just laugh at him. Miles goes to get me a water and him another beer. I don't want to drink and drive; and I don't know anyone well enough to stay the night. Allison would so kick my ass for that one.

"Damn, girl, you got moves," Macie says as she greets me.

I blush, I can't help it. "Thanks."

"Here you go, sweetheart," Miles says, handing me a bottle of water.

I twist open the cap and down half of it. I barely have the cap back on before Macie is pulling me back out to dance. The four of us dance most of the night. Kaden got his turn, of which he bragged about. He can kid all he wants, but I know he has a thing for Macie. She even admitted that they've hooked up a few times.

As patrons start to pass out, I take that as my cue to leave. I hug Miles and Kaden and tell Macie I will see her at school the next day. The three of them walk me to my car and we agree to get together again soon.

The drive home is quick. I let myself in the condo, lock the door, and send a quick text to Allie.

**Me:** Just got home, hitting the shower then bed. Love you, guys!

I don't wait for her reply. I need a shower and my bed. My ass is beat, but I had fun tonight. I'm glad I went.

# ~ 23 ~

# *Aiden*

I break down the last box to take it out to the garage. Two days and I'm finally unpacked. It would have been sooner, but we spent the majority of the day yesterday at the store. We needed everything. Food, dishes, all that shit. We left everything back in Chapel Hill for Hales. Hales...I miss her. It's weird to be here knowing that she's not with us, that she's not going to just pop around the corner. She and Allison made plans for her to come down in a month. Four fucking weeks before I see her again. *Fuck my life!*

I finish putting my empty boxes in the garage and join Liam and Allison in the living room. I get there just in time to hear Allie tell someone to have a good time and be safe. *Is she talking to Hales?*

"What's she up to?" Liam asks.

"Not much. She met a girl in her assisting class today that invited her over to her house for a small get together. She just wanted someone to know where she was, you know, just in case."

"What the fuck! Does she not feel safe there? Why is she going then?" I blurt before Liam can even respond.

"Yeah, what he said," Liam replies.

"Yes, she feels safe. It's a new place and new people. Hales and I made a pact when we started college that we would never go to a party alone. I left her," she says quietly. "I'm really proud of her for being responsible."

"Text her and tell her that we need to know that she makes it home safe," Liam says.

"Already done, papa bear," Allison says, patting his cheeks. "She promised to text me as soon as she's home."

Liam grumbles, but I'm not sure what he's saying. My mind is racing with the thought of Hales not being safe. I stalk off towards my room. I can't let them see me lose my shit.

Once in my room, I begin to pace. My every instinct is telling me that I need to go to her now. I need to go to that damn party and make sure she's okay, make sure all those fuckers know that she's mine.

No, I know I can't do that, but I want to. I continue pacing and running my fingers through my hair. I need to learn to deal. This was my choice to not pursue a relationship with her. My fucking choice that is driving me in-fucking-sane!

"Ace?" I jump at the sound of Allison's voice. She is standing in the doorway of my room.

"Knock much?" I spit. I immediately feel like shit for snapping at her. "Sorry, Ash. What's up?" I try to act calm when I'm anything but.

She smiles at me knowingly. "We ordered pizza. Liam and I are too tired to cook, and I assumed that you would be too," she tells me.

"Thanks, that sounds fine," I say. Not really thinking about food. I sit down on the edge of my bed and rest my elbows on my knees. Focusing on breathing in and out, in and out.

I feel the bed dip beside me as Allison rubs her small hands up and down my back trying to sooth me. She knows. "You know, Ace, she's going to be fine. Hailey is a smart girl. She did the right thing by calling and texting me the address."

My heads pops up at her words. "You have the address. You know where she is?" I ask, standing up.

Allison is shaking her head no. "You are not going after her, Aiden Emerson. You made your choice, now you have to deal with it," she says sternly.

"But...What if..." She holds her hand up stopping me.

"She's fine. What are you gonna do? Drive three hours to drag her from a party to leave her there alone again. She has to live her life, Ace," she tries to reason.

"Fuck!" I sit back down on the bed and place my hands behind my neck. "If anything ever happens to her..." I can't say anymore. I can feel the emotion building in my throat.

Allison leans in for a hug. "Everything is going to be fine, just relax. She promised to text me when she gets home." With that, she walks out of my room.

I lie back on the bed and stare at the ceiling. Allie's right. Hales has to live her life, but it tears me up inside to think about it. To think about her being alone and all those guys falling all over her. Even if we were together, she would be there in school and I would be here. Without her. I'm flipping the fuck out now. I can't imagine how it would feel if she really was mine.

I must have been lying there for a while because Allison knocks on the door yelling that the pizza is getting cold.

I make my way to the living room and see Liam and Allison are curled up watching a movie. The pizza boxes are on the coffee table. I sit down and begin to eat. Allison smiles. "There's a bottle of water for you on the table too," she says.

"Thanks." I resume eating without conversation. I just finish my last piece when I hear Allison's phone ping notifying her of a new message. My heart begins to race. Is she home, is she okay?

My eyes bore into Allison as she reads the message. "She's fine. She just got home, says she going to take a shower then go to bed," Allison tells us.

I feel myself relax a little, but I need more. I need her to tell me she's fine. I clean up the mess of the pizza boxes and tell the lovebirds goodnight, before heading to my room. I make a beeline for my phone and send her off a quick text.

133

**Me:** You're home safe?

I hold my phone to my chest, willing it to notify me that she has replied to my message. I wait three minutes and no reply. That's not like her. What if someone has her and they sent the message to throw us off. I send another message.

**Me:** Angel?

I wait another three minutes and still nothing. My heart is pounding in my chest. I pick up my phone and tap her name in my favorites list. It rings four long agonizing rings, before I hear her sweet voice.

"Hello?" She says breathlessly.

"Hey, angel," I whisper. She answered. That's a good sign.

"Hey," she says softly.

"You're home safe?" I ask, getting right to the point.

"Yes, I was in the shower," she tells me.

We both sit in silence listening to the other breathe. I turn off my light and crawl into bed. Hales will be the last thing I hear before I fall asleep.

"I was worried about you," I finally say.

"I'm fine," she whispers. "Macie, she's a girl in my assisting class who is also in the RN program, she and her twin brother had a party. There were only about thirty or so people."

"Did you have a good time?" I ask her. I just want to keep her talking.

"Yeah, it was fun. We danced and just hung out really."

"Danced? Were you drinking?" I ask.

She laughs softly. "No, Aiden, I wasn't drinking. I'm smarter than that."

I release a ragged breath. "I know you are, angel. I just worry about you. So how many guys did you dance with?" I ask, trying hard for my voice to show no emotion at the question.

"Just Miles, he's Macie's twin. His best friend Kaden tried to get me to dance as well, but he was drinking pretty heavy and I just met them all, so yeah. I just didn't want to get myself in an uncomfortable situation."

"I'm proud of you, angel," I tell her.

"Thanks," she says in her soft sweet voice.

Again, silence but it's not uncomfortable. It's like neither one of us want to hang up. We stay quiet for several minutes before Hales says three little words that penetrate my heart.

"I miss you," she whispers across the line.

The ache in my chest is there, beating like a drum. How am I ever going to survive this?

"I miss you, too, angel," I say. What I really want to say is, I want you here with me now. I'm on my way to get you. You can transfer schools or just quit, I don't give a fuck as long as you are with me every day!

Hailey yawns and I realize I'm keeping her up and she has class tomorrow. "I'll let you get some sleep. I just needed to hear you tell me that you were home safe and sound," I say.

"I'm here, tucked into bed, in my new room."

I chuckle. "That's right. I was picturing you on the futon, but I guess you have upgraded with the place all to yourself. You know you have your own room here now too," I tell her. "So are you living it up having Liam's room all to yourself?" I ask.

"Uh, well, I um…I'm not in Liam's room," she says softly.

She's not? "You're not?" I asked, stunned. "That's the bigger of the two rooms."

"I just wanted to feel close to you," she mumbles sleepily.

*Holy Shit!* "I miss you so much, angel. Sweet dreams," I tell her. This girl has me by the fucking balls and she doesn't even know it. I can't believe she's sleeping in my room just to feel close to me. I remember her sweet words at the beach house when she told me she loved me. Does she want me the way I want her?

There's silence on the other end of the line, no reply from her, but I can hear her gentle breaths through the line. She's fallen asleep. I smile and burrow under the covers and let Hailey's soft breathing lull me to sleep.

I wake the next morning to my hand vibrating. I open my eyes and see that I have my cell phone clutched tightly in my hand. It all comes back to me. Hailey. My hand vibrates again. Rubbing the sleep out of my eyes I swipe the screen and see that I have a new text from her.

**Hailey:** Sorry I fell asleep on you last night. In class all day, will call later. XOXO H.

I ended and began my day with Hailey. The only thing sweeter would be if she was here in my warm bed, in my arms.

After a quick stop at the bathroom, I head to the kitchen for some food. I find Liam and Allison already awake and sitting at the table eating pancakes.

"Morning," I say, my voice still rough with sleep.

"Good morning. I made pancakes," Allison says, pointing to a plate piled high.

"Thanks," I say as I sit down at the table.

"So, we could do June," Allison says to Liam.

"No, beautiful, I told you I can't wait that long," Liam says, shaking his head. "Here, let me see the calendar."

Allison hands him her phone and he scrolls through the dates. He begins tapping on the screen before he hands it back to her with a smile.

Allison looks down at her phone and then back up at Liam. "That's the Saturday after the Super Bowl."

"Yes, it is. That is as long as I'm willing to wait. The only reason I agree to that is because I want to be able to take you away on a honeymoon."

Allison looks back down at her phone. When she lifts her head, she is grinning from ear to ear. "So we're getting married on February 8th?" she asks as if she can't believe it's really happening.

I can't help but grin right along with her. She deserves happiness, they both do.

"We're getting married," Allison screeches as she jumps out of her chair and launches herself at Liam.

He throws his head back laughing as he catches her. He gently places his hands on her cheeks. "I love you, beautiful girl," he says before he kisses her.

I smile before I say, "Uh, guys, I'm trying to eat here." They break away laughing.

"I have to call Hales," Allison says, reaching for her phone.

"She's in class all day," I tell her.

She and Liam both turn to look at me. "How do you know?" Allison asks.

I shrug my shoulders, like it's no big deal. When really it's a big fucking deal. "I called her last night to make sure she was okay. She mentioned being in class all day today. Well, the next two weeks eight to five, she will be in class and then clinicals." How do they not know this? Hailey mentioned it before we left also.

"All right, well, I guess I'll be calling her at five," Allison says.

"Let's go call my parents and tell them," Liam says.

I finish my huge stack of pancakes and then clean the kitchen. I decide to go out and pick up a few things. Training camp starts next week, and even if I'm able to find the time, my ass is gonna be dragging.

# ~ 24 ~

# *Hailey*

The first two weeks of class have flown by. I'm really enjoying it, which has me even more excited to start the nursing program in a few weeks. Life is crazy as well. Liam and Allison set a wedding date, so Allie and I have been spending our evenings on the phone and FaceTime starting to make plans. She is setting up appointments for when I come and visit at the end of the month. Just two more weeks.

I have also been spending a lot of time with Macie, Miles, and Kaden. We have hung out at their place a few more times as well as going out to dinner, a dance club, and a frat party. The guys are great and remind me a lot of Liam and Aiden. Kaden is head over heels for Macie and she him, but they're fighting it. Well, not completely. When they are both drinking, they usually end up hooking up, but neither one of them are ready to make it official. Miles treats me just like Macie. He has even gone as far as trying to hook me up with a friend of his. I declined. This, of course, led to an intense conversation about Aiden.

"Who is he," Miles asks me one night at a frat party after I turn down all of his suggestions of male companionship. When I don't answer, he continues. "Hailey, you're hot as fuck. Any guy would be lucky to have you. You have every guy in this place panting after you and you couldn't care less. Who is he?" Miles asks again.

"He's no one," I say, not meeting his eyes. I can feel the blush creep up my face just at the thought of Aiden.

"Come on, Hales. Let's you and I take a walk," Miles says, placing his arm around my shoulders and leading me outside to the back deck. The frat house sits on what they refer to as "frat row." There are several fraternities who live on the street, and there is even what they refer to as "Frat Park" which is located at the cul-de-sac at the end of the street. Miles and I walk to the park and find it's deserted. No alcohol is allowed at the park; the cops patrol it regularly. They would love to get a group for public intoxication. So really, it doesn't get much use. Well, not at nighttime anyway.

Miles leads me to the swings and we each take one. "Okay, girl. Spill it. Who is he and what the fuck is wrong with him that he's not with you right now?" he says blatantly.

"It's...complicated."

"Explain it to me," Miles prods.

I run my shoe through the sand, moving back and forth. Maybe getting a guy's perspective would help. Miles doesn't know Aiden, so he can be objective. I take a deep breath and words just start spewing out of my mouth.

"His name is Aiden. He's my brother's best friend. Hell, he's one of my closest friends as well. I have loved him for as long as I can remember," I say in a rush.

"Okay, so how does Aiden feel about you?" he questions.

I shrug my shoulders. "He doesn't know," I mumble.

"What? Did you just say that he doesn't know? As in, he has no clue that you're in love with him?" he asks, shocked.

"Yes," I whisper.

"Why? Is it your brother? What's keeping you from telling him?" Miles is determined to understand.

I decide to unleash it all. I tell him about all the "little" moments, the touches, the few kisses that we've shared. I tell him about how good Aiden is to me and how he has told me several times since he left that he misses me.

"I just don't know if he feels that way about me. It's like one minute he does and the next he's backing away. I think we're just really good friends and he likes to flirt," I explain to Miles.

"What are you afraid of, Hales?" Miles asks quietly.

"What am I afraid of? I'm scared to death that he's going to reject me. That I will lose one of my best friends because I need more. The four of us, Allison, Liam, Aiden, and I, we're a tight group. If I pursue him and he rejects me, that's all going to be jeopardized. I can't be the one to break up our group. I want him. I'm in love with him, but I can't risk losing him and what we have. I won't. Besides, I'm just his best friend's little sister, he doesn't want me."

"Maybe he's afraid of what your brother will say," he suggests.

I laugh. "Liam has no leg to stand on with that one. Allison was my best friend and roommate before she got with my brother. Aiden also considers her to be his little sister, so Liam can't be angry."

"Do you want to hear what I think?" he waits for my reply. I simply nod my head. "I think you're making excuses. You have yourself convinced that you are and will always be just a little sister to him, and as a guy, I can assure you that he sees you. I don't know what's holding him back, but it's my guess that it's the same thing that's holding you back. He's probably afraid to break up the group if things don't work out. I think you're both letting fear of the unknown run your life."

"I need him to be a part of my life," I whisper into the night.

Miles is off his swing and crouched down in front of me in no time. "You can't live life in fear. You have to live and take chances. I suggest you tell this Aiden character how you feel. Tell him that if he doesn't feel the same way, you can go on as if the conversation never happened. He could be it for you, and you for him. You have to take the chance, Hales."

"Maybe…maybe I will. I need to think about what you've said. It makes sense, but I'm still scared shitless to lose him," I tell him, fighting back tears.

I stepped out of my comfort zone that night and opened up to Miles. Since then, I have also talked to Macie about Aiden, and because Kaden is always around, he knows as well. They all say I need to "take the chance". Of course, I throw Macie's words right back at her. All I ever get in return is a smile and an eye roll.

Tonight I'm venturing a little further out of my comfort zone. Macie, Miles, and Kaden are coming over to the condo to watch movies. It's Friday night and it's been a long ass week. Macie and I want to unwind, and Kaden usually ends up where Macie is, and Miles where Kaden is, so…I invited all three of them. Actually, all three of them have become really close friends and I would have invited them anyway. I just like to make the guys think that they are lucky to be included.

"So, what do I need to bring tonight?" Macie asks me as we walk to the parking lot.

"Just yourself, unless there is something specific that you want. I am just going to order pizza. I have chips and dip as well as pop and water. If the guys or you want alcohol, you will need to bring that. There needs to be a designated driver, otherwise, you all have to spend the night," I tell her.

"We would never drink and drive. That's cool of you to offer us to stay. I'll let the guys know. So we should be there around seven, sound good?"

"Yes, that's perfect," I say as I climb into my Fusion.

I rush home to straighten up and take a quick shower. I stopped at the store last night so that snacks are here. All I need to do is put them out and order the pizza. I miss Allison's call while I'm in the shower, but I don't have time to call her back. Everyone will be here in fifteen minutes. I have spent too much time online looking at wedding decorations. I think I'm just as excited as Allie and Liam. I have some ideas for her so I will call her back when we have time to talk.

At seven o'clock on the dot, I hear a knock at the door. I yell for them to come in. Immediately, my mind flashes to Liam and Aiden scolding Allie and I for doing that in our dorm room last year. I guess now that I live alone, that was not exactly the best decision. Note to self, always see who is knocking before saying come in, and keep the door locked.

I'm walking into the living room as they come through the door. Miles has a scowl on his face, as does Kaden.

"Hey, guys!" I say happily. I really am excited to see them.

"Hales, what the hell? You can't just yell for people to come in, and why the fuck was your door unlocked? You live alone, you need to keep that shit locked and always see who it is first," he scolds me.

I smile.

"This is not funny. What if it was some madman at the door," he asks angrily.

"I'm sorry, Miles. I'm not laughing at you. Liam and Aiden yelled at me for that same thing. You just reminded me of them, that's all," I say, sliding my arm through his and leading him to the couch.

I push Miles down onto the couch and Kaden plops down next to him. "Nice pad, Hales."

"Thanks. Here are the movies, or we could play Bullshit? Not sure if you guys are into cards?" I ask them.

"I also brought Battle of the Sexes," Macie says, sitting down on the recliner.

My cell phone rings, causing me to jump. I reach for it at the same time as Miles. I end up losing my balance. Miles reaches out, grabs me, and pulls me onto his lap, breaking my fall.

"He-hello?" I say, laughing.

"Hales? What's so funny?" Allison asks on the other end.

"Nothing," I say, still laughing. "Miles, stop it," I scold him.

"What? I'm not doing anything," he says, laughing at me.

"Hales, who is that? Is there a guy there?" she asks, surprised.

"What? No, I mean yes. It's just Miles. He Macie and Kaden are over just hanging out. I think I'm going to kick their asses in a game of Bullshit," I tell her.

"Bullshit!" Kaden yells.

All four of us bust out laughing. For some reason, we are all slaphappy tonight.

"Well, it sounds like ya'll are having fun. Call me tomorrow. I have some appointments booked I want to tell you about," she says.

"You can tell me now, we're just hanging out," I reply.

"No, you have company and it sounds like this Miles character is torturing you." She laughs.

"He won't stop tickling me," I say as I try to squirm away from Miles.

"Miles, st-stop it. Please, I have to pee," I cry.

Allison laughs. "Call me tomorrow, girl. I love you."

"Love you too, Allie. I'll talk to you in the morning," I say before hitting end on my cell.

I finally have both hands free to maneuver myself out of Miles's grasp. "You're evil," I say, running down the hall. *I really have to pee!*

# ~ 25 ~

# Aiden

Two weeks. It been two fucking weeks since I've seen Hailey. Two weeks without her smile, her silly jokes. Two long fucking weeks.

It's Friday night and the official end of our first week of training camp. My ass is dragging and so is Liam. Allison has been great. She is taking care of our tired asses. I'm stretched out on the loveseat while Allie and Liam are on the couch. Liam and I both decided that it hurts to move, so we don't.

I hear Liam chuckle. "What's so funny?" I ask him.

He laughs. "I feel like an old man. Here we are just graduated from college, and a night in on the couch is what we've been longing for," he tells me.

"Fuck, don't I know it. I don't want to move until I have to," I reply.

"Oh, you two, you're not old. Training camp for the NFL, that's huge. Of course you're going to be tired," Allison reasons.

"Did you get any appointments scheduled today?" Liam asks her. He has been hounding her every day to get the wedding planned. He told her to make it her dream wedding. All he needed was her. She and Hailey have been talking every night, planning. It's good to see her happy.

"Yes, actually I did. Crap! I forgot to call Hailey." She reaches for her phone on the coffee table.

I'm missing Hailey so much that I tune in on her conversations with Allison just to get a glimpse of what's going on in her life. She and I have texted a lot over the past two weeks and even talked a time or two, but nothing like the night I fell asleep with her. I haven't slept good since that night.

I can only hear one side of the conversation, but my interest is piqued when I hear Allison ask Hailey if there is a guy there with her. I sit up straight on the loveseat and stare at Allison. She has a smile on her face, so Hales must be okay with this guy being there. Who the fuck is he? Why is he with Hales? There are a million questions and scenarios running through my mind.

Allison calls the guy Miles. Who. The. Fuck. Is. Miles? She tells Hales to call her tomorrow and she loves her, and then hangs up.

"What's up with Hales?" Liam asks her.

Thanks, buddy, I owe you one. It's easier for him to ask the questions than me. They are both already suspicious of me and my feelings for Hailey.

Allison smiles. "Macie, the girl she met in class, and her brother are there. Miles was tickling her so much she couldn't stop laughing."

"Does she know these people that well? She must trust them if she's letting them come over and he's tickling her to death," Liam says calmly.

How the fuck is he calm about this? We don't know this dude and neither does Hailey. How do we know she's safe? I stand up because sitting just isn't working for me. My temper and my emotions are on high alert.

I'm pacing back and forth behind the couch and running my fingers through my hair. I look at my watch. It's seven thirty. If I leave now, I can be there before eleven. I stalk to my room, grab my keys, wallet, and phone. I make my way to the front door and have just slipped my shoes on when I feel a heavy hand land on my shoulder.

"What's up, man? Going somewhere?" Liam asks me.

*Shit!* How do I explain this? This need to keep her safe. How do I explain the ache that resides in my chest that grows more prominent each day that I'm away from her? How do I tell my best friend that I'm head over heels for his little sister?

"She doesn't know them, Liam. What if they try to hurt her? We're not there. We just left her alone. I'm going to drive up there and make sure she's okay," I tell him. Hoping he doesn't see right through me.

"Aiden, Hailey is smart. She would never intentionally put herself in that position. Allison said she was laughing and having a good time," he tries to reason with me.

"What if-" he cuts me off.

"Look, why don't you call her first. That way you can hear her tell you herself that she's okay," he suggests.

I don't answer him. I turn around and track back to my room. I close myself inside and hit speed dial for Hailey.

It rings twice before I hear her voice. "Aiden?" she says in question.

I suck in a breath at my name on her lips. "Angel."

"What's wrong? Is everyone okay?" she asks me, concern lacing her voice.

"Yeah. I was…" I clear my throat. I feel like I can't breathe. "I was just worried about you," I croak out.

"Worried about me? Why?" Confusion evident in her tone.

I gulp a couple deep breaths and try to calm down. "Allison said there was a guy over, and well, that's not like you and I was worried…I'm worried about you, angel," I say softly.

Hailey doesn't say anything, so I keep going. "I have my shoes on, keys in hand, and Liam stopped me. I was coming to you. Liam said that Allie said you were fine and I should call you and hear for myself," I pause. She still says nothing, but I can hear her breathing on the other end. "Do you need me, angel? I can be there tonight," I say, willing her to say yes, she does need me.

She clears her throat. "Aiden, I'm fine really. Miles and Kaden are great guys. They would never hurt me," she says quietly.

Two guys! What the fuck? I struggle to remain in control of my emotions. "Miles and Kaden?" I question.

"Yes. Miles is Macie's twin brother and Kaden is his best friend. They actually remind me a lot of you and Liam," she says.

If she's trying to make me feel better, she's not. If they are anything like me, they want her. Want her so much that it hurts to breath when she's not around. I don't feel like I have truly taken a breath in two long weeks.

Trying to reel myself in, I ask again "You're okay?"

"I'm fine," she whispers.

"Okay, but if you change your mind, if you need me, I'll be there. Please, call me before you go to sleep. I need to know your safe," I tell her honestly.

"Okay, I will. I really am fine."

"All right, then. Have a good time, be safe. I'll be waiting to hear from you."

"Talk to you soon," she says and the line goes dead.

I sit there on the edge of my bed and replay our conversation. She really did sound fine to me. It hits me that I totally freaked out in front of Liam. He has to be wondering what the fuck is wrong with me. At this point in the game, I don't really care if he knows. I'm ready to risk it all just to be with her. I know for a fact, with everything in me, that if Hailey ever truly becomes mine, I will make damn sure that she never wants to leave me. I will do whatever it takes to keep her in my life. The question is…am I too late?

There is a knock on the door. "Hey, man, you okay?" Liam asks through the door.

I stand up and pull the door open. Liam's standing there with his hands in his pockets looking at the floor. "Come on in," I say, sitting back down on the bed.

Liam enters and sits in the chair in the corner of the room. "How long have you been in love with my sister?" he asks.

At first, I don't answer, weighing my options. I think about the ache in my chest that gets heavier every day, the way everything is brighter when she's around. I look up at Liam and the look on his face tells me that I can't lie my way out of it this time anyway. "I don't really know when it happened. There isn't really an exact moment that I realized it," I tell him honestly.

"Are you going to do something about it?"

His question catches me off guard. He doesn't sound pissed, just curious. Fuck it, I'm all in at this point. "I don't know. I'm scared as hell to lose her, man."

Liam raises his eyebrow. "What do you mean lose her?" he asks.

"What if we get together and things don't work out. I can't imagine us being able to be just friends. I would never be able to handle another guy with her. Hell, look at me know. I'm a fucking mess because she has a guy at her place. She's says they're all just friends, but fuck, what if I'm too late?"

Liam doesn't answer right away. He seems to be thinking about how to say what he wants to say. Or maybe he's just thinking about how he's gonna kick my ass. "I know I struggled for weeks about pursuing Allison. I knew in my gut that she was special, that she would be different from anyone else. I fought that because I was scared. Scared that giving up the freedom of being single would somehow ruin things for me. Man, I was so fucking stupid. Life with Allison is amazing. I know that every day for the rest of my life I get to wake up next to her. I know that if my day sucks, all I have to do is see her and it's suddenly better." Liam chuckles.

"What's so funny?" I ask him.

"I was just thinking about Gran, and her letter to Allie. The one that inspired her tattoo. Live and Love Fearless," Liam says.

I don't respond, because really, what else is there to say? I'm letting my fear of losing Hailey completely control what I really want. Her.

"Listen, man. I can't think of anyone that I would rather see my baby sister with. If it's me that's keeping you from seeing where things go, then you have my blessing," he says as he stands up and holds his fist out to me.

We fist bump and he leaves me alone in my room, my head swirling with our conversation. Liam was a big part of the reason as to why I never pursued anything with Hales. He just gave me his blessing. *Holy shit!* I never thought that would happen. Now I just need to decide if I can risk losing her if things don't work out between us.

# ~ 26 ~

# *Hailey*

I hit end on my cell phone and lay it on the kitchen table. When I saw the screen light up with Aiden's name, I came in here for privacy. I can't believe he was on his way here. He really did sound worried about me.

I hear footsteps. I look up to see Miles enter the kitchen. He settles into the chair next to mine. "Everything okay?"

"Yeah, um, that was Aiden. He was worried about me. He overheard my conversation with Allison and he was concerned that you and Kaden are here. He had his keys in hand, almost out the door, when my brother stopped him from leaving. Liam told him to call me so he could see for himself that I'm okay," I explain.

"Wow! Dude has it bad for you, Hales."

"Yeah, right. He's just used to taking on the big brother role. It gets harder and harder to not let these small things that he does affect me and my feelings for him. It's hard for my heart to get the message that we're not together. He's just being nice."

"Whatever you say, girl. I'm a guy, I know how guys think. He wants you and he's fighting it," he tells me. "So, are you okay?"

"Yes, he wants me to call him before I go to bed, so he knows that ya'll didn't kidnap me or anything."

Miles laughs. "Yep, dude is crushing hard," he says as he tugs on my arm and pulls me behind him back to the living room.

The night is fun. I really like hanging out with the three of them. However, I'm distracted most of the night. I know they all notice, but not one of them mention it. We play battle of the sexes and I keep zoning out. Poor Macie, she has to pick up the slack. Thankfully, we still pull off the win. We play Bullshit and I laugh so hard I almost piss my pants. Kaden keeps cheating and Miles is helping him. Macie just pouts about holding so many cards. It's been fun, but I'm tired and ready for them to go. None of them have been drinking, so they are good to drive. I just want to call Aiden back.

"Sleepy?" Kaden asks Macie.

"Yeah, I'm ready to go," she tells him.

Kaden nods his head and starts cleaning up. Those two should just call a spade a spade and make it official.

"Thanks for having us," Macie says. "I had a great time. I'm just exhausted." She yawns.

"I get it, trust me."

"Well, we're out. The living room is all tidied up. Make sure you lock the door behind us," Miles says.

"Always, thanks for coming, guys."

I follow them to the door, say goodbye again, and then secure the lock. I walk through the condo turning off lights. I'll get the rest of the mess in the morning. I grab my cell off the coffee table and head to bed.

I quickly change for bed, brush my teeth, and climb under the covers. No matter what the temperature is outside, I have to have a cover to curl up in. I pick up my cell and hit my speed dial for Aiden.

"Angel," he says on the first ring.

"Hey. I'm all tucked in safe and sound. Everyone just left a few minutes ago," I tell him.

I can hear him exhale and I smile. He really was worried. "I'm glad. Did you have a good time?"

"Yeah. They're fun to hang out with. I think you guys would really like them," I say. Aiden mumbles something under his breath. It sounded like "I doubt it," but I can't really tell and I don't want to ask him. It doesn't really matter anyway.

"So how is training camp?"

"Good, it's kicking my ass, but I love it."

"I'm really proud of you and Liam. You guys both deserve this," I say sincerely.

"How about you? Classes ended today and next week you start clinicals, right?"

"Wow, I'm impressed you remember. Yes, class is over. I passed my final exam, now all I have to do is pass clinicals, and nursing school here I come," I laugh.

"That's awesome, Hales. I'm so fucking proud of you."

"Thanks," I whisper.

"Thanks for calling. I would have worried all night. Get some sleep."

With that, he hangs up and I lie there staring at the phone. I don't know what's going on. Things feel different between Aiden and me. Our relationship has slowly been changing. I used to think it was all me, but since he's been gone, he's been more concerned and protective of me. I don't want to get my hopes up, but it feels like he might want more.

I sleep in on Saturday, which is why I'm jolted out of bed at ten o'clock to my cell phone ringing in my ear.

"Hello?" I mumble into the phone.

"Morning, sunshine," Allison says, way too damn chipper for a Saturday morning.

"I have so much to tell you. First of all, we'll be coming home, well to Chapel Hill, next weekend. Your mom wants to throw a small engagement party. There really won't be much time during the season with away games, and since the wedding is right after the

Super Bowl, she wants to do it this weekend. Just close friends and family. I can't wait to see you," she says in a rush.

"That's a great idea. Mom mentioned it to me the other day, but she didn't say when she was thinking. I think she's just as excited as you are about the wedding."

Allison laughs. "I know, right? She and I talk several times a day. Speaking of that, we also have a cake tasting coming up. I'm going to try and plan it for the weekend that you are here in Charlotte visiting. Your mom found a great catering company that will travel to Chapel Hill if that's where we decide to have the wedding." Allison takes a breath. "I'm getting married!" she squeals.

I laugh at her excitement. "Yes, and soon you'll be my sister. You're the best decision Liam ever made," I tell her.

"Aww, I love you too, Hales."

"So when is this shindig going down?"

"It's Saturday night at seven at your parents' house."

"Awesome. What can I do to help?"

"Nothing, your mom is amazing and she has taken care of everything. I just need my maid of honor and best friend there with a smile," she says. "Your mom also told me to have you invite Macie and her brother and his friend. I forget his name." She laughs.

"Kaden. Okay, I'll see if they have anything going on. I really would like for you to meet them. I think you and Macie will hit it off," I tell her.

"Well then, extend the invitation and we can add them to our family."

"Done," I laugh. Allison has no living relatives so we really are her family. Soon we will be for real; she's going to be my sister! "I'm really excited to see you guys. I miss you like crazy."

"Us too. I know Liam and Aiden miss you just as much as I do. I can't wait for you to spend the week with us."

"All right, well, I need to drag my ass to the shower and wash my scrubs for next week. Let me know if anything comes up that I can do. Oh, by the way. Are you guys staying here with me while you are home?" I ask. I chew on my lip waiting for her answer. I want them here. I miss them.

"We really haven't talked about it. I'll check with the guys and get back with you," Allison says.

"Sounds good. I hope you do. I really miss you!" We say our goodbyes and I drag myself into the shower with a smile on my face. My peeps are coming home!

# ~ 27 ~

# *Aiden*

Finally! It's Friday. This week took for-fucking-ever to pass. I feel like I did when I was younger waiting on Christmas or my birthday. This is better; this is the day I get to see Hales. It's been three long-ass weeks since I've laid eyes on her.

Liam and Allison broke the news to me Sunday night.

"So, we sort of have a favor," Allison had said.

"What's up?"

"Well, Liam's parents are throwing us an engagement party next weekend and we really want you to be there since you are the best man," she says hopefully.

The first damn thing that popped in my head was Hailey. I get to see Hailey. I should have thought, "Oh, I can swing by and see my parents" or some responsible shit like that. Nope. Not me. My first and only thought was Hales. How much I miss her and how this was going to be one of the longest fucking weeks of my life waiting…wanting.

So, here we are, piled up in my new Tahoe. Well, new to me. It's a used model, low mileage. No need to go crazy, well, not yet anyway. Allison started dragging things out to the truck the minute Liam and I got home from camp today. She is so damn excited for this engagement party. Well, and to see Hailey. Not only did my mind think of this day nonstop for the past week, but Liam and Allison both talked about it as well. We're all excited to see her for three different reasons. Liam, of course, wants to see his sister and Allison her best friend. Me, well, I get to see my heart. The girl that holds it anyway. I had hoped that time away from her would help me expel these feelings, it's done the complete fucking opposite. All I do is think about her.

I replay my talk with Liam, the one where he told me that I have his blessing. That's a major obstacle out of the way. Now, the only obstacle is me. I want more with her. I fucking want all of her, but does she want me? Can I give into this temptation to call her mine and make it work? Can I honestly risk losing her being a part of my life if things don't work out? Hell, can I handle seeing her with some other douche bag? *Fuck!* I can't think about that without getting pissed off.

I shake my head, as if that will clear the image of her with someone else. I realize that we are finally pulling into the city limits of Chapel Hill. It hasn't even been a month, and yet it feels like a lifetime. Allison had asked us if we wanted to stay with the MacCoy's or with Hales. Of course my vote was to stay with Hales, as was Allie's. Liam was out voted. Well, not really, we knew we were the majority and didn't really care what his vote was. I missed my girl and I plan on spending every fucking spare minute with her this weekend. I need my Hailey fix.

I pull into the lot and quickly remove my seat belt. I fling open my door and pop the rear glass. I hear Liam mumble something about me "acting like a lovesick fool," well, yeah, I am. It's been three very long weeks without seeing her smile or having one of her hugs. The tightness that has been heavy in my chest the past few weeks eases with every step closer to her door. I raise my hand to knock, since, well, I don't live here anymore. Before my knuckles can connect with the door, it's flung open and Hailey is standing in front of me smiling.

I suck in a breath at the sight of her. She's so fucking gorgeous. Her long dark hair is loose around her shoulders, and those blue eyes are sparkling with happiness. Her lips, pink, plump and ready to be kissed. I clench my bag tighter with my left hand and place my right hand in my pocket. I have to restrain myself from grabbing her and kissing her until we're both breathless. *My angel.*

Hailey squeals and throws her arms around my neck. Instinctively, I drop my bag and wrap both arms around her. I hold her tight. I lean down and bury my face in her neck. Fuck me, she smells like heaven. "I missed you," she whispers.

I pull back and bring my hands to caress her face, gently stroking my thumbs across her cheeks. "I missed you too, angel. More than you know," I tell her. I want to kiss her so fucking bad. Thankfully, Liam and Allison step up behind us before I forge full steam ahead. Hales greets them with as much enthusiasm as she did me. I'm okay with that though. I know how much she loves Allie and Liam.

After a round of hugs, we drag our bags and our tired asses into the condo. Allison and Hailey scurry to the living room to talk wedding plans. Allison has a huge ass binder that she tugs around with her. She says it's going to be a small affair, but by the size of that binder...I'm not so sure.

Liam simply goes along with anything she wants. He says anything that makes her happy will make him happy. I chance a look at Hales, and yeah, I get it. I can see me being the same way.

"So, where do you want us?" Liam asks Hailey.

Her eyes go big and I see a blush creep up to cover her cheeks. What's that about?

"Well," she chews on her lip, "you and Allie can take your old room. Aiden, I have you set up in yours as well, and I will take the futon," she says as she points to the corner of the room.

"You took Aiden's room?" Liam asks. Shocked that she would choose the smaller of the two rooms.

I'm watching the interaction and her blush grows deeper. She's embarrassed. "Like she would want to sleep in the room where we had to hear you two lovebirds in all the damn time," I say, coming to her rescue. I make a mental note to ask her about the room selection. Hailey looks relieved that I spoke up.

"Yeah, I can still hear it." She pretends to shudder. "I decided Aiden's would be the safer bet. Less nightmares," she teases.

Now it's time for Allison to blush and I can't help but laugh. "You know she's right, Ash," I tell Allison.

Liam laughs with us as he pulls Allison into his side and drops a kiss on her head. "I love you, beautiful girl," he tells her.

I roll my eyes at Hales and smile. She offers me a smile in return as she says, "I see some things never change."

"Nope, not with these two." I motion my head towards the lovebirds.

"Well, I ordered pizza. It should be here any minute." Just as she says that, the doorbell rings.

She smiles and shuffles to the foyer to get the pizza. Remembering my manners, I jump off the couch and follow her so I can pay, or at least pay her back. She doesn't need to be paying for our food. I got this.

I reach the foyer and stop dead in my tracks. Some big-ass dude covered in tattoos has my girl in a hug. No fucking way! Who is this guy? I look around and don't see any pizza boxes. I clear my throat. Hailey turns and faces me, her face crimson with embarrassment.

"Oh, Aiden. This is Miles. He's Macie's twin brother. Miles this is my brother's best friend, Aiden," she introduces us.

Tattoo guy offers me his hand. "Nice to meet you. I've heard a lot about you," he tells me.

"You too," is my reply. I can't take my eyes off his arm that is thrown over her shoulder. I hear a low chuckle come from tattoo guy, Miles, and he tightens his hold on Hailey. She doesn't appear to be uncomfortable and she doesn't make any effort to have him move his hand. Is she with him?

Hailey turns to Miles. "So what brings you by?"

"Right, I brought your clothes by that you left at my place the other night," he says with a wink as he hands her a bag of clothes.

What. The. Fuck!

Hailey blushes. "Thank you. You didn't have to do that. I could have got them another time."

"It's not a big deal, sweetheart. I wanted you to have them in case you needed them," he says, pulling her tighter against his side.

I'm just standing in the foyer, trying to control my anger. I have no right to be pissed. I did this. I decided the reward didn't outweigh the risk. I made the decision for us to remain friends. I'm the one who is too chicken shit to tell my dream girl, that she's that, the girl of my dreams, the most important person in my life, because I'm afraid to lose her. And now…well, now I get to watch some other dude claim her as his. My night just went to shit.

# ~ 28 ~

## *Hailey*

Allison texted me about ten minutes ago and said they had just hit the city limits. I'm pacing back and forth in front of the living room window, waiting for them to arrive. Finally, after what seems like way longer than ten minutes, even though I know it wasn't, I see them pull in. Allison had told me they were in Aiden's new Tahoe and that it was white. I watch as Aiden jumps out of the driver side, grabs his bag, and takes quick long strides to the front door. *God, I missed him.*

I run to the foyer and throw open the front door. Aiden has his hand in the air ready to knock. I launch myself at him. I feel his arms wrap around me and I sigh and hold tighter.

I hear Allison and Liam join us and I attack them with hugs as well. This is the first time in the last three weeks, I really feel like I can breathe. I have missed these three so much. I'm afraid that saying goodbye on Sunday is going to kill me. It will definitely be worse than the first goodbye. My heart now knows how it feels to be so far away from them.

I usher them into the house and Liam asks what the sleeping arrangements are. *Shit!* I knew this would be brought up, with me insisting that they stay here and all, but I thought I would at least have a few minutes to get myself together before I had to announce that I'm in Aiden's old room. There is no way that I can tell them the real reason why. I wanted to feel close to him. My emotions are all over the place, seeing them, seeing him. Being in his arms. I can't

163

think fast enough to come up with an alternative answer. As if Aiden can read my mind, he speaks up and saves me. He jokes about me having nightmares about what Liam and Allie had done behind closed doors in that room. *Thank you, Aiden!*

I go along with the excuse, thankful that he stepped in and saved me. It's believable enough and we all laugh about it.

The doorbell chimes, and I grab my wallet to pay for the pizza. What I find is Miles.

"Miles, hey!" I say, surprised to see him. They all knew that I was busy tonight.

"Hey, Hales. How are you?" he says, bending down to give me a hug.

"Good, actually. Liam, Allie, and Aiden just got here. I thought you were the pizza guy," I say, releasing him from the hug.

I hear someone behind me clear their throat, and I know, before I even turn around, who it is. Aiden. I can feel him. I slowly turn, face flushed with embarrassment. I don't know why; it's not like I was doing anything wrong. Beside, Aiden and I are just friends. I can hug who ever in the hell I want. My heart needs to get on the same damn page as my brain.

Miles throws his arm over my shoulder as I quickly make introductions. They shake hands; it appears to be reluctant on Aiden's part. Needing to break the tension, I look up at Miles and ask him what brings him by?

To further increase my embarrassment, he hands me a bag of clothes that I left at their place earlier in the week. The four of us had went out to dinner right after class and I changed there. Instead of tugging my bag along, I left it there. It was late by the time we got back and I just got in my car and left. Standing here now, with Miles's arm around me holding me close and Aiden standing there looking like Miles just kicked his puppy, this situation looks a lot worse than what it really is. The way Miles said it sounds like I was there to spend time with him, intimately.

At this point, there is not much I can do to diffuse the situation. I don't want to make a scene, so I simply say, "Thank you," and take the bag from him. Miles is being really flirty and calling me sweetheart. This is something that he does, but he seems to be really laying on the charm tonight.

Miles tucks me tighter into his side. I see Aiden's jaw clench and he shoves his hands deep in his pockets. His eyes capture mine for a long pause before he turns and walks away.

As soon as he is out of earshot, Miles releases me and holds his hand up for a high five. I slap his hand, not sure, what we are celebrating.

"He's jealous," Miles says, grinning.

"He...what?" I'm confused. He thinks Aiden is jealous and he's happy about that?

"Just what I said. Your boy is jealous, which is exactly what I was going for," he says with a wink.

I just stand there staring at him with my mouth open. He was trying to make Aiden jealous?

"Look, Hales, with everything you've told me, it's clear he wants you. He's fighting it. I know you're tore up over this guy, so I thought maybe if he thinks he has a little competition, it might motivate him to take what he wants, which is you," he explains.

"We're just friends," I whisper, still in shock that Miles planned to make Aiden jealous.

"Bullshit! That guy wants you. He's pissed off thinking you and I are together. I plan to do this all weekend. That is, unless you insist that I don't. Kaden, Mace, and I talked about this last night. Aiden has never had competition before. He or Liam always ran them off before you had the chance to pursue anything, right?"

I shake my head yes.

"Well, now that they are gone; you've met new people. It's not our fault if they get the wrong impression." He shrugs like it's no big deal that Aiden thinks he and I are together.

"Miles, I..." he stops me.

"Let's just try it and see what happens. I want to see you happy, and I don't think you will truly be until you are with him. So, I want to help make that happen. Let's just let it play out, okay? You don't even have to lie to him. You can tell him that we are just friends. He will believe what he wants, because he's tore up about it. He wants you, but thinks you're mine."

I stand there in the foyer, torn. Do I do it? Do I let Aiden assume that Miles and I are an item? No, I will deny it. I can't lie to him. "I won't lie to him."

"I'm not telling you to lie to him. I'm asking you to trust me to make him see that you are what he wants, and that he's not willing to stand by and let another man take what's his."

"I don't know…"

"We're not lying to him. We're just giving him the nudge he needs to take the next step," he says, squeezing my arm. "I'll see you tomorrow night." He turns to leave and then turns back around with a smile. "Pizza's here." And he walks away.

I see the delivery guy walking towards the door. I go through the motions of paying for the pizza and giving him a tip. Taking a deep breath, I walk into the living room with a smile on my face. I'm acting like nothing happened, that Miles didn't suggest that I had spent time at his house intimately, and that Aiden didn't get pissed off and leave us there.

"Hey, guys, sorry it took so long. Miles dropped by to give me some things I left at their house, and then the pizza guys showed up," I say, holding up the boxes before placing them on the table.

"Aiden said a friend dropped by, but he failed to tell me it was a guy. What the hell, man?" Liam says to Aiden.

Aiden shrugs his shoulders and opens one of the pizza boxes.

"It was just Miles. He's Macie's twin brother. He'll be at the party tomorrow night, so you all can meet him then," I tell them.

Aiden's head snaps up and his eyes meet mine. I can't read his expression. He turns his head and continues eating.

"So, this Miles character? Are you guys together?" Liam asks me.

I shake my head no. "He's just a friend. He, Macie, and Kaden have become close friends of mine. I pretty much had to start over when you all left," I say softly.

Liam is up out of his chair and wrapping his arms around me. "We are just a few hours away. I'm sorry we had to leave. I know this has been hard on you." He drops a kiss to the top of my head. "I can't wait for you to spend the week with us. Who knows, you'll be done with school in a year. They hire nurses in Charlotte," he says with a wink.

I love my big brother. He's always there no matter what even if he lives three hours away.

I wiggle out of his arms and grab a slice of pizza. I don't want their time here laced with sadness. I only get them for two short days, and I want to enjoy that time.

"All right, Allie. Spill the deets on the wedding. What do you have planned for my visit?" I ask my best friend.

Just like I hoped it would, this forged the conversation ahead, and wedding planning is in full swing. Allie busts out her wedding binder and we go over the details of cake tasting, dress shopping, and food tasting. I focus all of my attention on her and her special day. I feel like I'm missing so much even though I talk to her every day. It's just not the same.

After we polish off two large pizzas and an order of breadsticks, we are all full and ready for bed. I insist that Aiden take my bed, but he refuses. Liam and Allison lock themselves in Liam's old room. I can't help but smile. Although temporary, our group is back together where we belong.

# ~ 29 ~

# Aiden

I'm lying here in the living room of our old condo, Hailey's condo, on the futon that was hers for when she would stay over. The blankets and the pillows smell like her. I'm surrounded by her. Hailey is in my room, in my bed. Well, my old room and my old bed, but it's fucking with me knowing that she's there, surrounded by me. As if that is not enough to keep me awake, every time I close my eyes, I see that Miles character with his arm around her.

It took more will than I knew I could summon to leave her alone with him in the foyer earlier tonight. I was so excited to see her, to spend time with her, but after seeing them together, I kept my distance. The girls spent the majority of the night talking wedding details while Liam and I watched ESPN. That's really all we had the energy for anyway. Training camp is hard work, and then the drive up here. I'm tired as hell, but I can't sleep because all I see is him, with his hands on her.

Eventually, exhaustion takes over and I fall into a restless sleep.

I woke up this morning to find Hailey and Allison already out and about. Liam is sitting on the couch watching television eating pop tarts.

"Thought you were going to sleep all damn day," he says, shoving in the last bite of his breakfast.

"What time is it?"

"Ten. The girls went to get a massage and manicures. You and I are gonna head over to mom and dad's to help set up for the party. Allie and Hales will meet us there later," he tells me.

"All right, man, let me grab a shower."

"Pack your clothes for the party, who knows what mom will have us doing." He tries to act annoyed, but I can hear the softness in his voice.

I rush through a shower and pack up my clothes for tonight's festivities. It's not formal, but clean clothes after working all day will be nice. Just as I'm zipping up my bag, Liam yells "heads up" and chucks a pack of pop tarts at me. "I made breakfast," he says with a smile.

As soon as we pull into the driveway at his parents' house, his mom is waiting for us on the porch with a clipboard in her hand.

"Shit, look at her. She's going to be a slave driver today," Liam groans.

"Well, we better get started then," I say, climbing out of my Tahoe.

I greet Mrs. MacCoy with a hug, as does Liam. She immediately starts going over what still needs to be done. "I'm so glad you guys are here. The crew is almost finished setting up the tent. Your father is on his way back with tables and chairs; those will need to be set up." She looks at her list. "We still need to hang the lights in the tent and bring fire wood to the pit just outside the tent. We have two large coolers that need to be stocked with ice and beverages, but not until later, I don't want the ice to melt before people even get here. The caterer will be here at five to set up and begin grilling. Your father and I wanted to enjoy the party instead of spending out time cooking," she says as we stand there and try to take in everything she's telling us.

"Mom, take a breath," Liam laughs. "We got this, okay? This is supposed to be just a small gathering to celebrate Allie and me. Everything is going to be great." He tries to calm her.

"Oh, and we need to set up a table for the DJ. Don't forget to remind your father when you help him set up," she says, completely ignoring Liam's little speech to calm down.

Liam sweeps in and lifts her up in the air, giving her a huge hug. "Mom, I love you. This is going to be amazing. Relax," he tells her.

"Put me down. I have work to do," she scolds him, laughing.

Mr. MacCoy pulls in and we immediately get to work setting up the tables and chairs before we tackle the rest of her list. I keep checking my watch, wondering when the girls are going to get here. Liam has talked to Allie a couple of times. They are at the condo getting ready and will be here by five thirty. I'm willing time to move faster.

We finally finish our "to-do list," with just enough time to shower and change. As I enter the kitchen, I hear voices and I know the girls have arrived. I clear the bottom step and look up. What I see stops me in my tracks. Hailey. She's dressed in a white sundress, her hair is loose and flowing down her back, and she's wearing pink flip flops. Her freshly painted pink toes draw my attention. Who am I kidding? Everything about her draws my attention.

I realize I'm standing there, staring at her like an idiot. I will my feet to carry me into the room and take a seat at the table beside Allison. She leans into my shoulder as a hello, but never breaks her conversation with Mrs. MacCoy. I pull my phone out of my pocket and scroll through my e-mails. There is nothing there that can't wait, but I need a distraction before I embarrass myself.

My distraction works, I'm only brought out of my trance when Liam taps me on the shoulder. I look up and realize that he and I are the only ones left in the kitchen. "Where did they go?" I ask.

He laughs. "Dude, you were in the zone. People are starting to get here, so they went outside. Come on, this new guy, Miles, and two others are here, and I need to go check them out," he says, walking out the back door.

*Fuck!* I hope he keeps his hands to himself. I can't take watching them together all night. Who am I kidding? The five minutes last night just about sent me over the damn ledge.

I pull myself out of the chair and follow Liam. I know this night is going to be torture. I know Miles won't be able to keep his hands off her. Hell, if she was mine, I wouldn't either. Hales denies that there is anything more than friendship going on there, but she has to know that any red-blooded guy would want her, all of her. *Fuck!* This is going to be hard to watch.

I stop at the bottom of the deck where Hailey is introducing everyone. There is another guy, Kaden, and the girl, Macie, who is with Miles. They all look to be just friends, until Miles spots me. He smirks and moves closer to Hales, gently moving her hair off her shoulder. She looks over and smiles at him, and I can feel my chest crack with pain. I'm too late. I'm glad the MacCoy's stocked up on alcoholic beverages, I have a feeling that's the only thing that is going to get me through tonight.

Hailey introduces me and I nod my head. I know it's a dick move, but that's all I can manage. Instead of sticking around, watching her being pawed by him, I walk away. I find Mrs. MacCoy and see if there is anything she needs me to do. Maybe if I stay busy, I can hold off on my alcohol consumption and be distracted enough to not have to see them together.

"Aiden, where is everyone?" Mrs. MacCoy asks.

"Hailey is introducing them to her new friends. I just wanted to see if there was anything you needed done."

"No, I think we're all set. You can sit and keep me company for a few minutes if you like," she says, pulling out the chair beside her.

I smile at her and take a seat. "You know, they really are just friends," she says softly.

*Holy shit!* Am I that easy to read? "Who?" I play dumb. I know she can tell that I'm pretending not to know who she's talking about. This is not the distraction I was hoping for.

"It will all work out. Just have faith," she tells me.

Before I can respond, I see a shadow and look up to find all of them. Hales and her new friends along with Liam and Allie. Great, just fucking great.

"Oh good, you're all here. I want to start the night off with a dance, and since Hales and Aiden are the entire wedding party, I want the two of you out there too," Mrs. MacCoy says.

I jump up out of my seat and round the table to stand beside Hailey. Miles is standing close to her, too close. At least he's not touching her. I slip my fingers through hers and she turns to look at me, shock on her face. "Dance with me, angel," I say as I gently tug on her hand, pulling her out onto the makeshift dance floor. Allison and Liam are already there, lost in each other. I pull Hailey as close to me as I can get her. I couldn't care less who sees, this might be my only chance to hold her tonight and I'm taking full advantage.

Hailey immediately rests her head against my chest as we gently sway to the music. My hands are resting on her hips and I pull her tighter. I don't want to be able to tell where she ends and I begin. I need her snug against me. My heart is beating a thunderous rhythm. I know she has to be able to feel it with the way she's laying on me. As if she can read my mind, she lifts her head and places her hand on my chest, right over my heart. She looks up at me with those beautiful blue eyes.

"Aiden," she whispers.

I lean my forehead against hers. "That's all for you, angel," I say softly as I hold her stare. I'm willing her with my eyes to understand what she means to me. How much I care about her. She has to be able to feel it, this connection.

Hailey is the first to look away as she rests her head back over my heart. She places both arms around my back and squeezes me tight. I feel her release a deep breath and relax against me. She's just as affected as I am. I don't know how much longer I can do this, resist her.

The song ends and I feel a tap on my shoulder. It's Miles. "Care if I cut in?" he asks, already reaching for Hailey. She quickly steps away from me and joins Miles in the next dance, a slow dance.

I stalk back to the tables, stopping to grab me a couple beers. Yes, I said a couple. I've lost her. I may affect her, but she's found someone else. I waited too long. Hence the multiple beers. I'm definitely going to need liquid courage to get through this night.

# ~ 30 ~

# *Hailey*

Miles cuts in at the end of my dance with Aiden. I sigh with relief. I was about two seconds away from making a fool of myself in front of my entire family. Anymore time wrapped up in his arms with his sweet words, and I was going to throw caution to the wind and make a move. Every time we are together, the electricity between us flows to the point that I can't think clearly. Aiden is always so tender and sweet. I want, with everything in me, to believe that he wants to be with me. Maybe we've both fought it for so long, that we don't know how to change it.

"I love it when a good plan comes together," Miles says in my ear. I'm sure to an outsider it looks like he's whispering tender words into my ear, not the true reality of him gloating that he was right about Aiden. "You should see him. He went straight for the cooler and grabbed a few beers. He does not like you in my arms," he says as he drops a kiss on my temple.

*Holy shit!* Miles is stepping up his game big time. "I may need a few of those to get through this night as well. One minute he is there, sweet and caring, making me think that he does want us, want me. The next, he's off throwing back a few beers trying to forget it ever happened."

"He's fighting it. Trust me. He's convinced that you and I are an item and that pisses him off. Keep denying it because that's the truth. However, in Aiden's eyes, I'm holding his girl. To him, that is the only validation needed to confirm we're together." The song ends

175

and Miles bends down to whisper in my ear again. I'm sure the moment looks intimate. "Trust me," he whispers, grabbing my hand and leading me off the dance floor. We stop at the cooler and Miles hands me a beer. Yep, I am so going to need liquid courage tonight.

My dad walks up behind us. "You staying here tonight, baby girl?" he asks.

Luckily, my parents are cool with my drinking even though I am still a year from legal drinking age, as long as I stay here tonight. This is a special occasion after all.

"Yes, dad. Allie and I brought our bags in earlier," I say, reaching up to give him a hug.

"Just making sure you're safe," he says, squeezing me back and walking away.

Miles leads me back to the table with his hand on the small of my back. He even pulls out my chair for me. I avoid looking at Aiden. Miles sits next to me and scoots close. He gently lays his arm on the back of my chair. I focus on my beer. Macie engages me in conversation about how great of a couple Liam and Allison are. I agree with her. I hear Aiden ask Liam if he needs another beer. I chance a look and see him walking away from the table.

Mom comes around and tells us it's time to eat. We join the line at the food table and fill our plates with way more food than we can eat, well, at least the girls have. Liam, Miles, and Kaden are doing just fine. In fact, they each finished off what Allie, Macie, and I couldn't. It's been a while since I have seen Aiden. I mention it to Liam and all he says is, "He's around here somewhere."

The sky has completely fallen dark and the tent is lit up with stands of white lights that give off an enchanted romantic glow. I watch Liam and Allison on the dance floor, completely caught up in each other, not caring at all what's going on around them. Miles scoots back his chair and offers me his hand.

"Let's give them a little competition. They're playing our song," he says as the song turns fast. I laugh because it's the first song that he and I ever danced to on the night I met him, Aerosmith's "Walk This Way."

I've had several beers and I'm feeling relaxed. Luckily for me, my grandparents have left and it's just the younger crowd. My parents are around, but I don't see them. Miles and I are about to get our groove on. As soon as we reach the dance floor, Miles spins me so my back is to his front and wraps his arm around my waist pulling me tight. I begin to move my hips to the beat. I place my hands above my head and behind his neck; this prompts him to bury his face in my neck. I hear him whisper, "Aiden is in the back corner, watching our every move." Me in my inebriated state decide that I want to give Aiden a show. Show him what he's missing. I push against Miles and I hear him groan in response. I can't help the smile that breaks across my face. At least someone is affected by my moves. Miles spins me to face him and our hips begin to grind back and forth. His arm is tight around my waist and my hands are resting on his shoulders. I tilt my head back and let the music dictate my movement. This also brings my chest front and center for Miles' viewing pleasure.

I'm lost in the music, so I don't realize that Aiden is standing beside us until I hear his voice. "I can take it from here," he growls at Miles. With that, he grabs my hand and tugs me into his chest. Miles holds his hands up in the air and steps backwards as if to say he doesn't want any trouble. Aiden crushes me to his chest and places his knee between my legs. I begin to sway my hips to the beat, as does Aiden. It didn't feel like this with Miles, just Aiden. Only Aiden. I can feel his hardness against my leg and I bite my lip to surpass the moan that I feel on the tip of my tongue. Aiden tugs me tighter, if that's even possible, and rocks his hips against mine. My hands are around his neck, and I run my fingers through his shaggy brown hair. His face is buried in my neck as he traces his tongue from my collarbone to my ear lobe. I shudder. I can't help but wonder if it looks as erotic as it feels.

The music changes and turns slow as Dierks Bentley's "Breathe You In" begins to play. Aiden pulls me close and I bury my face into his neck, doing just what the song says...breathing him in. I can smell his cologne and the alcohol on his breath. Apparently, he needed liquid courage to get through this night as well. We are barely moving to the music. We are simply wrapped in each other's arms enjoying the moment. I'm trying to memorize every second, every single detail. I reach up and kiss him softly on the neck, the taste of his skin exploding on my tongue. I hear Aiden growl and that just adds fuel to that fire that has ignited between us. I tug on his hair bringing his lips to mine. Somewhere in the back of my mind, I know that I will probably regret this in the morning, but right now in this moment, I can't find it in me to care. Aiden sucks in a breath, shocked; I'm sure that I'm molesting him. Instead of pulling back, I take the opportunity to slip my tongue past his lips. He presses me tight against him; his hardness now rests against my belly as he takes control of the kiss. I break away needing to catch my breath and rest my head back against his chest. I hear him take in a breath as his hands find my hips. The song is coming to an end and I don't want to let him go. I want Aiden more than I have ever wanted anything.

I feel Aiden pull away. He lifts my chin with his forefinger and kisses me on the forehead. He leans down to whisper in my ear, "Take a walk with me, angel?"

My heart is racing and I'm stunned speechless. Aiden wants to be alone with me. I thought for sure as soon as the song ended, he would run away from me as fast he could. I can't believe I just attacked him on the dance floor. Embarrassment takes over and I am unable to form words. I nod my head yes. That's all the answer he needs as he laces his fingers through mine and gently leads me out from underneath the tent and into the darkness. He leads us to the pond. Aiden sits down in the grass, and I follow him. He reaches over, grabs my hand and laces our fingers together again.

"I can't seem to stop touching you," he tells me, his voice thick with emotion.

"I don't want you to," I reply. I'm more open than usual due to the amount of alcohol in my system. I never would have admitted that had I been sober. Lucky for me, I'm also too wasted to care. I want him. I've always wanted him. "The night is beautiful. Look at the stars."

"I can't think of a better background," he tells me. "Can you do something for me, angel?"

"Anything," I say. It's true; I would do anything for him.

"Will you let me hold you? I just want you back in my arms so damn bad."

"Yes." The word is barely across my lips before Aiden is scooting back and placing his legs on either side of mine. He places his hands around my waist and pulls me back against his chest. He moves my hair to the opposite shoulder and places a feather soft kiss to my neck. I relax into him at the feel of his lips against my skin.

"Fuck, Hales, I miss you so fucking much it hurts."

I don't say anything, because I can't. I try to swallow the emotion in my throat. I feel hot tears prick the back of my eyes. I turn my head in effort to keep Aiden from seeing me cry. I'm losing the battle. His words undo me. I've wanted him for so long, and I love him with everything in me. Now, here we are, and my drunk ass is crying. I turn my head up and try to focus on the night sky. The stars are so bright tonight.

Aiden gently grips my chin to turn me back to him. He lifts me up and sets me sideways in his lap. "Hailey, baby, what's wrong? Why are you upset?" he asks, tugging me closer to him.

"I just…I just really miss you too," I say. What I want to tell him is that I'm in love with him. He's the first thing I think of when I wake up and the last before I close my eyes. I want to tell him that I've been afraid that he would always see me as only Liam's little sister, and treat me as such. Although, right now, in this moment, he doesn't seem to be treating me like a little sister.

Aiden leans in to kiss my cheek and I turn my head, our lips collide. Instead of pulling back, he freezes, his lips still pressed against mine. I pull away and turn to straddle his hips. He cups my face with his big hands. "Hales?" he whispers.

I lean down and press my lips to his. I trace my tongue across his lips, teasing him, begging him for entrance. Aiden growls and deepens the kiss, opening his mouth and allowing our tongues to dual in their pursuit of each other's taste. I'm lost in him, his taste, and the feel of him between my legs. All of it. I'm utterly and completely lost in Aiden.

He slows the kiss and rests his forehead against mine. "Baby, are you sure. You've had a lot to drink tonight and so have I. I don't want you to regret this." I can hear the concern in his voice.

"Will you regret this?" I ask him.

"No. Never could I ever regret a minute spent with you, let alone you in my arms. No, I won't regret this. But I'm worried that you will," he tells me.

Instead of saying anything else, I rock my hips against his as I lean down and capture his lips with mine once again. He has both hands on my hips, assisting me with rocking back and forth across his erection. I feel him, all of him. All that separates us is my panties and his cargo shorts. I've never done this. I've never been with anyone. I've kissed guys and there has been touching, but not like this. I've never straddled a guy and rocked my hips to a rhythm that is driving me insane. I feel pressure building and I realize this too is new. I've never had an orgasm. Aiden is about to give me my first.

I break away from the kiss and throw my head back, continuing to rock back and forth against Aiden. He runs his hands up under my dress and gently unsnaps my bra. I feel his hand slide under the cup and he gently caresses my nipples. "Aiden," I whisper.

"You are so fucking beautiful, Hailey." He removes his hand and tugs the top of my sundress down, revealing my breast. He latches on to my nipple as he gently caresses the other. The feel of his mouth on me is what sets me over the edge. Sensing that I'm close, Aiden lifts his head and crushes his lips to mine, swallowing my screams of pleasure. *Holy shit!*

He slows the kiss and eventually trails kisses down my neck as he finds his way back to my breast. He gently kisses one, and then the other, before he runs his hands back up under my dress. Tucking me back into my bra, he then reaches around and snaps it back into place. Once he's finished righting my clothing, he wraps his arms around my waist and buries his face in my chest. His grip is tight, but I embrace it. I want nothing more than to be exactly where I am, where we are.

I gently run my fingers through his hair, just allowing him to hold me. Enjoying my post orgasmic bliss. "Thank you. That was a first for me," I tell him softly.

Aiden pulls back. "What do you mean a first for you?"

I can feel the heat rush my face. Thankfully, it's too dark for Aiden to be able to tell. I hope. "That was my first, well, you know."

"Baby, you've never had an orgasm?"

"Not until you. Never had anyone kissed my breasts either," I say. Shit, the alcohol is causing me to be a damn motor mouth.

"You've never...I was your first?"

"Yes," I say, feeling embarrassed. Before Aiden can dissect what we've just done and what I've told him, his cell phone shrieks into the quiet night.

He digs in his pocket and pulls out his phone. "It's your mom," he tells me before sliding the screen to answer her call.

"Hello?" he says into the line. He's quiet, and then I see his jaw clench. "Yeah, we went for a walk. We'll head back now," he says, hitting end on his cell phone.

"Your friends are leaving and want to say goodbye to you," he tells me.

"Okay." I start to remove myself from his lap, but he stops me.

Aiden gently rubs his thumb over my bottom lip. "Lips of an angel," he breathes, and then kisses me one last time, soft and sweet. "Let's go say goodbye to your friends," he says, offering me his hand to brace myself to stand up. I tug him up and he envelopes me in a hug.

With that, we walk back towards the tent hand in hand. Smiles broad across both of our faces. When we are almost back to the tent. Aiden stops, which halts me as well. He gently rubs his thumb across my knuckles of the hand he's holding. "I'm going to let go of your hand, not because I'm ashamed of you or what we did, but I don't know where your head is with all of this. I need you to know that it meant something to me. You mean something to me," he tells me.

"There you two are." Aiden immediately drops my hand at the sound of my mom's voice. "Hales, your friends are ready to go and want to say goodbye."

"Right behind you," I say as I follow her back into the tent. I assume Aiden is behind me. When I reach the tent, Miles, Macie, and Kaden are waiting on me. Miles smiles broadly as he looks over my shoulder. I try to subtly shake my head to let him know that he can stop the charade, but he doesn't seem to get it. He rushes to me and engulfs me in a hug. Before I can stop him, he's pulling back and dropping a kiss to my lips.

"Fuck this!" I hear Aiden say behind us.

I push Miles off me and turn to watch Aiden storm out of the tent. "Shit!" I turn back to Miles. "What the hell are you thinking? I told you I didn't want to lie to him. Why did you have to kiss me? Now, he really does think that you and I are together. He wants me. You were right, but now...now, I doubt he'll ever speak to me again," I yell at him.

Miles reaches out for me, but I slap his hand away. "Don't touch me!" I yell at him. This apparently gets my brother's attention; he comes rushing to my side.

Liam wraps his arms around me. "Shh, what's happened, Hales? Did this guy hurt you?" he asks me, anger lacing his voice.

I pull away from him. "Liam, you have to go find Aiden. He left. He's upset. Please, you have to find him. He's been drinking," I plead.

Allison hugs me and tells Liam to go. "I'll stay with her, go find Aiden." With one last look, Liam turns to go find his best friend.

"Hailey..." Miles tries to talk to me, but I stop him.

"Don't. Just go, please. I need to talk to Aiden when he gets back, and it will only make it worse if you're still here," I say through sobs. "Please, Macie. I'll call you guys tomorrow," I beg her.

"Okay, since I know Allison is with you, we'll go. Promise you will call me tomorrow." She hugs me tight. "I'm sorry he did that. Miles really was just trying to help you."

I nod my head. Macie, Miles, and Kaden leave me alone with Allison. "What the hell is going on?" she asks me.

"Allie, he hates me." I cry harder. This sucks. We were finally getting somewhere and this happens. Shit. Shit. Shit.

"Tell me what happened," she says gently. So I do. I tell her everything from Miles's crazy plan to Aiden and me down by the pond. I don't leave anything out, I need her on my side. I need Allie to talk to Aiden and tell him that it wasn't what it looked like.

# ~ 31 ~

# *Aiden*

I dig my fingers into the palm of my hand, confirming I'm awake, that this is not a dream. Hailey and I really did just share the most erotic moment of my life. Not that anything we did was out of the ordinary; it just felt different with her. She's different. I've fought my feelings for her until I have literally driven myself crazy. Dancing with her tonight, holding her in my arms, the fight left me. I want her, have for a while, and I don't want to fight it anymore. I've never felt this way. Ever. I will do everything in my power to make it work, because she's mine now. There is no going back from this. I was pissed earlier, seeing her with Miles, but she swears they're just friends. Hailey has never lied to me.

When we are just outside the tent, I pull on her hand to stop her from going any further. I need to tell her what I've just worked out in my head. I need to explain to her that tonight was important to me, that she is important to me. Hales isn't just a hook up. I want her to be mine. I'm pretty sure she wants the same thing after what we just shared. I explain to her why I'm going to let go of her hand, and what we just shared is important to me, but before we can really discuss how she feels, her mom interrupts us. Good. I'm not too proud to admit that I'm jealous as hell of this Miles character. I want him gone. Hell, I want everyone gone so I can slip in some more alone time with my girl.

I follow Hailey into the tent, sporting a smile a mile wide. My mind is rewinding back the last thirty minutes, and I'm not really paying too much attention, until I look up and see Miles kissing Hailey. My Hailey. What makes it worse is that she is doing nothing to stop him. She's just standing there and letting him kiss her. She lied to me. My heart sinks and the smile on my face disappears.

"Fuck this!" I say as I turn and storm out of the tent. My mind is racing just as fast as my heart is beating. I can't believe she fucking lied to me! She said they were just friends. How could she have been with me, and then walk in there and kiss him? I want to rip his fucking head off, but really, why should I? Hailey made her choice. She doesn't want me. *Fuck!*

My first instinct is to get in my truck and drive away, away from Hailey and the pain in my chest. I've been drinking, and no matter how bad I need the distance, I won't ever drink and drive. Instead, I head back down to the pond and sit on the dock. I slip off my shoes and dangle my feet in the warm water. Now that I'm here, I realize this was not the best choice. I should have just went to the truck to sleep it off. Instead, I sit here staring at the spot where I touched her, kissed her. Fuck, this pain in my chest is intense. I've never felt this… this all-consuming need to…to not need love. Not even an hour ago, I was ready to go all in with her. I wanted her to know how I felt. I guess it's a damn good thing her mom interrupted us. *Son of a bitch!* I knew better. I knew I should have left her alone. It was a hell of a lot easier to want her from afar. Now that I've tasted her, witnessed her in the throes of passion…yeah, it fucking sucks ass!

I should have grabbed a few beers to bring down here with me, but then that would have required me to see people. I can't see people. I can just see Liam telling me how much of a pussy I am, crying like a baby over a girl. That's just it though, she's not just any girl; she's Hailey, and I thought she was my girl.

I see a shadow fall over the lake. I turn to see Liam sit down beside me. "Hey, man, you okay?"

"Fucking fantastic," my voice is laced with sarcasm.

"Care to fill me in on what happened?"

"You want to know what happened? I fucking fell in love with your sister. We went for a walk and had a…moment. I thought she felt the same way. I've been fighting this for months, and was finally ready to take the leap for her. Not two minutes later, she's kissing that fuckstick, Miles."

Neither, Liam or I say anything. The silence is there allowing me to run the image of Hailey and Miles over and over again, like a broken record.

"She's my Allison," I tell him, fighting the lump in my throat. "You don't have to worry about me breaking her heart though, because she just ripped mine out of my fucking chest."

"I think you should talk to her, she's pretty upset," he tells me.

I laugh. "Yeah, upset that she's busted maybe. Tell me what you would have done if you'd just decided to take the leap with Allie, and you thought she was on the same page as you, but then you walk into a room not two minutes later and see her kissing another guy. A guy she swore she was just friends with, but she isn't making any effort to push him away. What would you have done?" I question.

Liam is quiet for a few minutes. "I would have bolted. It took me a long time to decide to make a play for her, to let her see that she is what I want. I can tell you honestly, if I would have seen what you just described, I would have walked away too. I can't believe Hailey did that to you."

I don't reply, because I don't know how to. I really thought, after all these months of subtle touches and looks, she wanted me too. Hell, we just shared one of the most incredible moments of my life. She's good, I'll give her that. She sure fooled me.

Liam's cell rings. He pulls it out and shows me the screen. It's Allie. "Hey, baby. Yeah, I found him. No, he's not ready to talk to anyone right now. Let's just give him some time. I'm going to hang out here with Aiden for a while. Yeah, okay, love you too, beautiful girl," he says, hanging up the phone.

"That was Allison. She wanted to know if I had found you. She and Hailey wanted to come talk to you. I turned them away."

"Thanks, man. I can't see Hales right now, and Allison will just make me talk and I don't want to talk about how my heart just got ripped out of my chest. I'm done talking."

"I get it. So what's the plan?" Liam asks.

"The plan is that I'm going to sit my ass here on this dock until I'm sober enough to drive, and then I'm going home…to Charlotte. I'm going to try to forget her."

His phones beeps with a text. I watch as a smile spreads across his face. It has to be Allison. "What's she saying?"

"Oh, uh, she's heading upstairs to bed. She got Hales settled in and just wanted to tell me that she'll wait up for me."

"Go," I tell him.

"No, man, I'm good."

"Liam, go. I need time to clear my head anyway."

"Don't drive yet. Wait a little longer and text me as soon as you get there, no matter what time it is."

"Will do. My buzz is shot, so I should be fine in another hour or so. Hey, can you bring my bag with you tomorrow? I don't want to risk running into her. I know she and I will have to talk, but I just can't, not yet."

Liam stands to leave. "When you're ready, at least talk to her. Don't let this come between you guys."

Can I do that? I'm not sure. "I'll see what I can do. I can't promise anything," I tell him honestly.

Liam nods his head, turns and walks away. I'm alone again, with a steady reel of Hailey and I on repeat in my mind. Then I see Miles and his lips on hers, his arms around her. Hailey doing nothing to stop it, and the anger comes flooding back. *Fuck!*

I lie back on the dock and look up at the night sky thinking about what I could have done different. I think about the last several months and every single moment that I've shared with her. The signs were there, I just chose to ignore them. This is just as much my fault as it is hers. I should have told her how I felt. I should have taken a chance on her, on us. Instead, I pushed her to him.

My phone vibrates in my pocket; I pull it out and see a text from Hailey.

**Hailey:** Please let me know you're okay. I can explain. Please.

I stare at the message as if looking at it will tell me what to do. I close out of the message screen and see that I've been laying here for two hours. I stand up and stretch, all effects of the alcohol are gone. I pull my keys out of my pocket and head back towards the house to my truck. I don't really feel like driving back to Charlotte tonight, but I won't be able to sleep anyway, and I can't see Hailey. Not yet. I hit my key fob and unlock the doors. I climb in and go to set my cell phone in the console. I swipe across the screen with my thumb and open up her message.

**Me:** I'm safe. Don't worry.

I power off my phone and hit the open road. At least there won't be much traffic.

## ~ 32 ~

## Hailey

I toss and turn all night, worried about Aiden. I've checked his room three times to see if he has come back yet. His bag is still there. Liam said he just needed some time. I don't want to give him time. I don't want him to decide that what we shared was a mistake. Miles texted earlier telling me how sorry he is. I didn't text him back. I'm too angry and I'm afraid I will say something that I regret.

As the sun rises, light filters into my room. I jump out of bed and run down the hall to the guest room, Aiden's room. I quietly open the door and see that the bed is still made and his bag still sits there untouched. What the hell?

I walk across the hall and knock on Liam's door. Normally I wouldn't interrupt them, but I need to know where he is. He's had time to cool off. I need to talk to him. I hear Liam's mumbled "come in" so I push through the door.

"Hey, you," Allison says, sitting up. "How are you holding up?" she asks.

I shake my head no as I bite my bottom lip. Fighting back tears. "Liam, Aiden isn't in his room. I'm worried. I texted him last night to tell him to at least let me know he's okay. He texted back that he was safe, but he's not here and I'm worried," I mumble through the silent tears that are falling from my eyes.

Liam clears his throat. "He's not here. He went home last night."

"He did? Why didn't you tell me? I would have went to him. I need to tell him that what he saw was nothing. He misunderstood," I scold him.

"He went home to Charlotte," Liam says gently.

"Char-Charlotte?" I ask as a sob breaks from my throat. "Oh, God. He hates me."

Allison puts her arm around me. "He doesn't hate you. He's upset. Give him some time to cool off. You guys will work this out."

I crawl in bed next to Allison. I hear Liam tell her he's going to give us some "girl time," and he leaves the room. I'm too caught up in my grief to care. I'm so stupid. How could I agree to let Miles go through with his ridiculous plan? I should have ran after him. I let him walk away from me. I let the love of my life walk away. I didn't fight for him, now I can't. I finish my clinicals this week. I have to be there in order to start the nursing program. I sob harder at the thought of Aiden thinking I didn't fight for him, or that I won't fight for him. I want to go to him, but I can't abandon everything I worked so hard for.

Allison continues to sit with me through my tears. I love my best friend. "Thank you, for sitting with me. I'm okay now," I say, my voice hoarse.

"Give him some time. I know Aiden. He's angry and he needs to be alone to work through all of this. I can tell you that he's not over you. I've seen this develop with the two of your for months, and I've never see him with anyone the way he is with you. Just give him some time."

"I hope your right," I tell her.

My mom had made homemade cinnamon rolls before she and my dad left to return the tables and chairs. I'm relieved that I don't have to face them. We eat quickly then load up our stuff and head towards my condo. Liam pulls into the drive and turns off the ignition. Allison turns around in the front seat to face me.

"So, you're still coming next week right? I have a ton of things planned for us. I need you with me on this."

"Yeah, I'll be there, but maybe I should get a room. I'm not sure how Aiden will feel about me staying there. It's his house too," I tell her.

"Not gonna happen. You have your own room and Aiden will just have to deal. You two need to talk anyway, hopefully that can happen while you're there," Liam says.

"Okay," I say softly. Liam gets out and retrieves my bag from the back of his Pathfinder.

"Give me your keys and I'll take this in while you two say goodbye," he tells me.

I hand him the keys and turn to find Allison standing there with her arms open wide, waiting for a hug. "Trust me, this will work out. I'll see you in a week," she says, squeezing me one last time. Liam wraps his arms around both of us for a group hug.

"I love you, Hales. Everything will work out. You'll see." With that, he releases me and I stand there and wave as they pull away.

I make my way inside and it feels empty. I'm all alone again. I take a long hot shower and curl up with my kindle. I read until I can't keep my eyes open. I'm exhausted from no sleep the night before. I crawl into bed and sleep claims me.

I sleep clear through the night. Thirteen hours. I still don't feel rested. My emotions are draining me. I pull my hair up in a knot on top of my head, slip into some scrubs, brush my teeth, grab a granola bar, and hit the road. I'm dreading today because I'll see Macie. I know she feels terrible and so does Miles. He should. I told him it was a bad idea and that I wouldn't lie to Aiden. He took that out of my hands by completely catching me off guard. Miles is a good guy, but he has shit for timing. I can't blame him completely. I should have had the guts to tell him no and to tell Aiden how I felt. I should have followed Aiden and made him listen. Now I have to wait four more days to see him and try to convince him that he is who I want, always.

This week our clinical rotation is at a local nursing home. I pull into the lot and see Macie standing by the front door. I assume that she's waiting on me. Taking a deep breath, I grab my bag and climb out of my car. I walk slowly to the door. As soon as she spots me, she starts in my direction.

"Hailey, how are you? I'm so sorry that this happened. Miles feels terrible. Hell, I feel terrible. We both know how you feel about Aiden. I had no idea that he would take it that far. He said he was going to flirt and dance close to you, not attack you in front of him. I ripped him a new ass for you, multiple times. Kaden too." She stops, taking a deep breath.

"I'm okay, I guess. My heart hurts. I've wanted Aiden for years and when he finally says he has feelings for me, not Liam's little sister, but me, Hailey MacCoy, Saturday night happens."

"What can we do to help fix this? Miles is a mess," she asks.

I shrug my shoulders. "He won't talk to me. I'm going up there Friday night to spend all next week with them. I hope by me being there in the same house, he will finally give me a chance to explain. If not, well, I guess it wasn't mean to be."

"Don't say that. Everything will work out. I saw the way he looked at you. He's in love with you."

I laugh. "He wanted me, yes. Loves me, no. Hell, I don't even think he even likes me right now."

Macie smiles sadly as we walk through the doors to start our second and final week of clinicals. This is going to be one of the longest weeks of my life. I can't help but worry about Aiden, about our friendship. Wondering if there is any way he can find it in his heart to forgive me. I send up a silent prayer that he does. He's all I want.

# ~ 33 ~

# *Aiden*

This week has sucked donkey nuts! Coach has been riding my ass all week. I can't say that I blame him though, I deserve it. I can't seem to focus on anything, anything that isn't Hailey. I've had time to cool down, and I'm now pissed at myself for not punching that fucker and fighting for my girl. Allison and Liam both keep telling me that it wasn't what it looked like. They both keep urging me to talk to her. She's going to be staying with us for a week, and will be at our place tonight around eight depending on traffic. I plan to be in bed, or in my room at least, when she gets here. I don't want her first night to be ruined with us fighting. I want her to feel comfortable here.

"So, Hales should be here in a few hours," Liam says as we walk out of the stadium.

"Yep." I keep it short. I feel like he and Allison have talked me to death about her and what happened that night.

"You going to let her explain?" he asks.

"I'm sure we'll talk while she's here. Tonight, no. I want her first night with us to be pleasant. I'm going to hide out in my room. Haven't been sleeping too well this week. I need to get caught up." Lame ass excuse I know, but it's all I got.

"You don't have to do that, man. I know she wants to see you. She's scared as hell that you won't talk to her again."

I feel a ping of sadness in my chest that she's scared. I've avoided all her calls and messages since that night. I wasn't ready. "I promise we'll talk while she's here. Just not tonight, okay?"

"All right, man. Just let her explain," he says again.

As soon as we get home, I head straight to the shower. I rush through so I have time to eat and lock myself in my room. Allison comes in the kitchen while I'm making my sandwiches.

"Why are you eating when we're going out?" she asks me.

"I didn't know we were going out. I thought Hales was coming tonight."

"She is and we're taking her to dinner," she tells me, hand on her hip, just like my momma used to. I smile at her.

"Thanks, but I'm beat. Haven't slept much this week."

"You need to listen to what she has to say."

"I know, and I will while she's here. Not tonight. I'm exhausted and I don't have the strength for that kind of conversation," I tell her honestly.

She nods and I feel myself relax. I hate this. I hate that there is tension between all of us. I hate that no matter how bad she hurt me, I can still taste her. I can still feel her breath against my neck, the feel of her hips grinding against mine. I miss her like fucking crazy, but she made her choice. I know Liam and Allison say it was a huge misunderstanding, but I saw it with my own two eyes. They didn't see what I did. If they did, they would understand this pain I feel.

I scarf down my sandwich and a glass of milk. I say goodnight and retreat to my room. It's seven thirty. She will be here anytime. I can't deal with it tonight, but I have a feeling that I'll sleep better knowing that she's sleeping in the room next to mine, alone.

At eight o'clock I hear Allison squeal. Hailey's here. I hear voices and they get louder. They're in the hall outside my door.

"Is Aiden here?" I hear her ask.

"Yeah, he's exhausted. This week has been tough. Coach has been riding him. His focus has been shit this week," Liam tells her. At least he was honest without completely ousting me.

"I miss him," she says and it breaks me. I can hear the sadness in her voice and I want to fling open the door, pull her inside, and lock her in here with me. I want to rewind to last Saturday by the pond, when everything in my world made sense. When Hailey was in my arms and the thought of her being mine looked like a real possibility.

I hear Allison showing her around her room. The room that I furnished and decorated for her, to make her feel like this was her home, too. Anytime she wanted to be here, I want her to feel like she can be. I want her to know that she is still a part of us, even though we now live three hours away. I was so excited to show it to her. Instead, Allison gets to. She gets to see Hailey's face light up with happiness. *Fuck my life!* I hear their footsteps go back down the hall, and eventually, the front door closing. They're gone. I hope to be asleep by the time they come back, afraid the will to see her will be too strong, and I won't be able to resist.

I toss and turn for the next two hours, not able to relax. I hear the front door open. They're home. They talk for a few minutes and then silence. I hear Liam and Allie's bedroom door shut and I wait for Hailey's. I quietly climb out of bed and tip toe to the door and rest my ear against it. Did I miss it? It's then that I hear her soft voice.

"God, Aiden. I hope I can make this right. I hope I can make you understand. I can't lose you. I'm in love with you," she whispers. I hear her walk to her door. I hear her enter and close the door.

I stand there at my door shocked, confused, and angry. Too many emotions flowing through my veins. I slide to the floor and bring my knees to my chest as I run my fingers through my hair. She didn't know I could hear her. She thought I was asleep. She poured her heart out to my bedroom door. This is the second time Hailey has said those three little words to me. The first time, she was asleep and I wasn't really sure she knew what she was saying. There was large amounts of alcohol involved. Tonight, well tonight, she was wide awake. Her voice was soft and clear, no alcohol choosing her words for her.

I want nothing more than for her to love me. Love me as much as I love her. For the first time since that night, I feel hopeful. Maybe we can figure this out.

I get to my feet and drag myself to bed. I fall asleep quickly knowing that Hales is next door, safe and apparently she loves me.

# ~ 34 ~

# *Hailey*

I wake up to a quiet house. I use my private bathroom, brush my teeth, and make my way to the kitchen. There is a note on the counter from Allison.

> Hales-
>
> Went to run a few errands, I hated to wake you.
>
> I hope you got to sleep in. Liam and Aiden are at
>
> the gym.
>
> I should be home by ten.
>
> XOXO Allie

I look up at the clock and see that it's nine thirty. *Holy shit!* I never sleep this late. I grab a box of cereal from the cabinet and make myself a bowl for breakfast. Allison comes in just as I'm finishing up.

"Hey, you. Sleep okay?"

"Actually, yes. I've been up about ten minutes or so. So what's on the agenda for today?" I ask her.

"We have the wine tasting at seven. Liam and I have an appointment at the jeweler to look for wedding bands at five, so would you mind meeting us there? Aiden is meeting us there also. He's at the stadium most of the day. They're doing a tour for children with special needs and Aiden volunteered to be there for the meet and greet. Liam wanted to, but we have a lot to get done before the season starts," she explains.

My shoulders sag in defeat. It looks like I won't get to see Aiden and beg for forgiveness until tonight.

"The rest of the day is open. I thought maybe you and I could go to lunch and go shopping. You know, just hang out. I've missed you."

That sounds perfect. Let me grab a shower and then we can go."

I quickly finish off my cereal, rinse out the bowl, and place it in the dishwasher before scurrying off to the shower. I'm excited to spend the day with Allison. I've missed being able to just hang out with her.

An hour later, we are pulling into the local mall. Allison begins dragging me from store to store, and I can't help but smile. I really missed this. This is the first time I have smiled since the night I allowed Aiden to walk away from me. On the drive here, Allison told me not to worry, that everything would work out. She and Liam both told me that last night as well. I hope to hell they're right.

Allison does a great job of distracting me. I think we've hit every store in the mall. Okay, maybe not every store, but most of them. We, of course, hit the bridal shop, Victoria's Secret, and the jewelry store that she and Liam have an appointment at later, just to name a few. We eat a late lunch at the food court. All in all, it's a perfect day with my best friend. I needed this.

Allison drops me off at the condo. After she makes sure I have the directions to get to the wine tasting, she drives away. I have a few hours before I need to leave, so I decide to catch up on my reading. I don't know what is in store for Aiden and me tonight, but I hope he lets me talk to him. I hope he listens to what I have to say.

Allison said the wine tasting is thirty minutes from here, so at six fifteen I head out the door, giving me a few extra minutes in case I get lost.

I make it to the winery with no trouble. Gotta love the GPS! I park my car and make my way inside. I'm fifteen minutes early, but I can wait for the others inside. Once inside, I'm greeted by a lady in her late fifties or so.

"Good evening, dear. Do you have a reservation?"

"Yes. I'm here with the MacCoy – Hagan wedding," I reply.

"Wonderful. My name is Janice and I will be overseeing your party this evening. I have everything set up in a private room. There will be four in attendance, correct?" she asks nicely.

"Yes. I'm Hailey, the maid-of-honor, sister to the groom, and best friend to the bride," I say proudly.

"Good, just follow me and I will bring the others back as they arrive."

I follow her through a huge dining area filled with tables. Apparently, this is a restaurant as well. We reach the back of the room and enter a long hallway. At the end of the hallway there is a door, she opens the door to reveal a private dining room. There is a round table in the middle with place settings for four. On one wall, there is a table set up with an assortment of fruit, crackers, and cheese. On another wall, there is a table set up with several ice buckets and at least twenty different wines. Each one is labeled and has four small "sample" glasses, one for each of us.

"Wow, this is amazing," I tell her, because well, it really is.

"Thank you. Please make yourself comfortable and I will bring the rest of your party as they arrive." She leaves me.

I study the elegant paintings on the wall of different vineyards across the world. Allison really did her homework with this place.

The door opens and in walks Janice, followed by Aiden. My breath stills in my chest at the sight of him. He looks tired. His brown eyes that usually gleam with happiness are dull and sad. Regret hits me hard. I did this. I allowed him to think I wanted

Miles. Never Miles, always Aiden. I hope he gives me the chance to explain. I rub my sweaty palms against my thighs. It's been a while since I've been this nervous. Actually, I don't know if I ever have been this nervous. Everything I've ever wanted depends on if he will let me explain and if he believes me.

"Miss Hailey, your counterpart has just arrived," Janice says sweetly. "Mr. Aiden, please relax and take a seat. We can get started as soon as the bride and groom arrive." She swiftly leaves the room and here we are. Aiden and I alone.

Before either of us get the chance to speak, both of our phones ping with a message.

**Allison:** Hey, guys. Liam and I are stuck at the jeweler. Taking longer than we thought. Start without us. We trust you. XO A

"Shit," I hear Aiden mutter. Great, that doesn't sound like he's too happy to be stuck here with me.

"Aiden," I say softly. His eyes meet mine and I can't control the tears that begin to flow freely from my eyes. "Can we talk, please?" I ask as I wipe the tears from my cheeks.

He nods his head and takes a seat across the table from me.

Janice enters the room and I avert my gaze, so she doesn't see my tears. "I'm sorry but the bride and groom are detained. They have advised me to go ahead and start without them. Miss Allison has assured me that she will be fine with whatever the two of you choose."

Janice loads each of our plates with fruit, cheese, and crackers. She pours us both a tall glass of water and cracks open the first bottle. Aiden and I don't engage in conversation with each other. We simply taste the wine and answer Janice's questions about likes and dislikes.

Two hours later, stuffed full of cheese, crackers, and wine; I realize I'm beyond a little tipsy. "I don't think I can drive," I say to both of them, not that I expect Aiden to respond.

"Miss Hailey, you have nothing to worry about. Miss Allison and Mr. Liam arranged for one of our cars to drive you back home. They said you were all staying at the same place. Is that still the case?" she asks, obviously picking up on the tension between Aiden and I. "Either way, he'll take you wherever you need to go."

I look at Aiden, not sure if he plans to come home tonight or not. He addresses Janice. "Yes, we are still staying at the same place. Thank you, Janice." His voice deep.

"Good. Well then, I think I have all that I need as far as selection. I will notify our driver that you are ready to leave. If you would please follow me."

Aiden and I follow her down the long hallway through the dining room. There are a few people who recognize Aiden and yell out to him. He waves politely and smiles, but doesn't stop. We follow Janice outside and there is a limo waiting for us. The driver smiles politely and opens the door for us. Aiden motions for me to go first. I turn to Janice and thank her, and then slide in. I hear Aiden thank her as well, and then he makes sure the driver knows where he's going before sliding in next to me and shutting the door.

The privacy glass was raised when I got in, so it's just us. Alone. The tension is high, so thick you could cut it with a knife. I'm debating on whether or not I should try to talk to him now or wait until we get back to the house.

Aiden decides for me. "I know we need to talk," he says, his voice thick and low. "We will, I promise, but for right now, for the ride home," he clears his throat, "can I just...can I just hold you? Please?"

I hold my breath and nod my head yes. Aiden scoots closer and pulls me into his chest. I rest my head over his heart, and I can feel its steady rhythm as his chest rises and falls rapidly. He places a kiss on top of my head and tightens his arms around me. He doesn't say another word, and I don't dare ruin this. This may be the last time he ever holds me. Hell no, I'm not saying a damn thing. I release a breath and relax against him as I battle the tears that are, for the second time tonight, threatening to fall.

# ~ 35 ~

# Aiden

The last two hours have just about killed me. Watching Hailey and those lips tasting all that wine. I'm as hard as a damn rock. I may be angry at her, and myself, but I still want her, more now than ever before. I know how those lips feel against mine, how her skins tastes. The sounds she makes when she's coming undone in my arms. Like I said, it's just about killed me.

I slide into the limo and her scent engulfs me. The privacy glass is up. I'm not sure if Hales did that or if it was the driver. It's just us, and I'm scared to fucking death. I know she wants to talk, and so do I. I also know that Liam and Allison have been telling me all week that what I saw was taken out of context. What I don't know is if she wants me or him. I'm not ready to hear her tell me that it's him she wants.

I break the silence and tell her I know we need to talk and we will. Then my heart speaks before my brain has a chance to keep up, and I ask her if I can just hold her. My hands shake at the thought of her in my arms again. The thought that this could be the last time I hold her. I swallow back the lump in my throat and focus on my breathing to slow my racing heart.

Hailey nods her head yes and I feel my body relax just a little. I scoot closer to her and pull her down against my chest, wrapping my arms securely around her. I kiss the top of her head and hold her as close and as tight as I can. My mind keeps racing with the thought that this could be the last time. It's now that I decide, it doesn't matter what she says. I'm going to fight for her. I can't breathe without her. I'm irrevocably in love with this girl, and I can't let her walk away without a fight. I should have stayed and fought for her the first time. I won't make the same mistake twice.

The limo stops in front of the condo and I release the hold I have on her. She lifts her head and I gently stroke her cheek with my thumb. "We're home, angel," I say softly.

Her eyes well up with tears. "Aiden," she chokes out.

I crush her in a hug that I'm sure is painful for her, but I'm afraid of what we will become outside of the privacy of this limo. The driver opens my door, which means I have to release her. I grab her hand and lace our fingers together as I pull her out of the limo behind me. I tip the driver and thank him. Then I lead Hailey to the front door.

Just as we enter the door, I get a text for Liam.

> **Liam:** Hey, man. I heard you just got dropped off. Allie and I are staying at a hotel tonight. Take care of Hales and fix this shit. See you in the morning.

I chuckle. I never thought I would see the day that Liam voluntarily leaves me alone with his little sister, knowing that I want nothing more than to bury myself deep inside her. Well, I haven't told him that exactly. What I did tell him is that she's my Allison, so yeah, he knows.

I sit down next to Hailey on the couch. "That was Liam," I say, holding up my phone. "He said that he and Allie are spending the night at a hotel. He gave me strict order to 'fix this shit' and said they would see us in the morning." I wait to gauge her reaction. She's biting on her bottom lip, which is sexy as hell.

Without looking up at me, she asks, "Are you ready to talk now?"

Am I ready? No, I'm so fucking scared that she's going to choose him that my insides are twisted. "Yeah, I guess we need to," I say softly.

Hailey looks up and her eyes lock with mine. "What you saw," she takes a breath, "it's not what it looked like."

"Really?" I say, trying like hell to hold back the sarcasm in my voice. By the look in her eyes, I failed.

"Really. Aiden, I would never do that to you. You told me right before you walked away from me that what we shared meant something to you, that I meant something to you. My mom interrupted us before I could respond."

She turns sideways on the couch and I do the same, we are now facing one another. I grab a pillow and place it on my lap so I can hold onto it. I'm hoping the distraction will keep me from touching her. I really just want to touch her, hold her.

"Before I tell you what I would have said before we were interrupted, and what I'd hoped to tell you later that night before you walked away, I need to start at the beginning."

"We've got all night," I tell her.

"Miles was trying to help me." She wrings her hands together, and I can hear a slight quiver in her voice. She's nervous. "Macie, Miles, and Kaden all three have become fast friends of mine. The first night I met Miles, he hit on me, but I didn't take the bait. He asked me who *he* was. He wanted to know who the guy was that held my heart." She stops to collect her thoughts. She reaches out, grabs one of my hands and places it on her lap. She laces her fingers through mine. I instantly feel myself relax just from her touch. "I laughed it off, and we continued to dance and have a good time. The next time we hung out, that same question was asked again. I'd had a few drinks. I wasn't drunk, but loose and I couldn't hold it in anymore. I had to tell someone."

"Tell them what, angel? Did someone hurt you?" I ask her. I'm confused as to where she's going with this.

She smiles at me, and I want to lean in to kiss those lips. "No, no one hurt me. But I've sorta had a thing for this guy for as long as I can remember, and it's hard to keep it in and not talk to anyone about it. I figured since none of them knew the guy, I could open up and talk about him, about how I fell head over heels in love with him and was too afraid to tell him."

I try to pull my hand away, but she holds tight. "I thought you said Miles was helping you. How the fuck is he helping you by kissing you like that when you…when you love someone else?" I barely choke out the last words. I'm sick at the thought of her with someone else.

"I'm getting there. Just hang with me a little while longer. So, I open up to the three of them and they all agree that the guy in question really does have feelings for me. He's just too afraid to show it due to our mutual acquaintances. Miles got this crazy idea to flirt more and try to make the guy jealous whenever he was around. He thought if the guy thought he was losing me, he would step up and make his move."

"I'm still a little lost here, angel," I tell her. My mind is racing. Is this other guy me? If not, who? "Was this guy there on Saturday night?" I ask, trying to work this out in my head.

"Yeah, he was." She smiles at me and grips my hand a little tighter. "He actually asked me to go for a walk with him down by the pond. Turns out that he has, or had, feelings for me too. We shared the most earth-shattering experience of my life. He gave me a first for the history books. He was gentle and sweet, and then we were interrupted by my mother."

I can feel the back of my eyes burn. All the emotion from the last week is swirling inside of me. She's talking about me. All I want to do is grab her and kiss her until we are both breathless, but I hold off. I need to hear everything she has to say, and if I kiss her now, there will be no more talking. "What happened next?" I say, my voice hoarse and thick with the love I have for this girl.

"Well, we headed back to the party and he stopped me outside the tent. He told me that what we shared was special to him, that I was special to him. Before I could say anything else, my mom interrupted us. I wasn't too worried though, because after I said goodbye to my friends, I planned on telling him exactly how I felt."

"How do you feel?" I ask softly, my eyes never leaving hers.

Hailey sits up on her knees and leans towards me. She takes both of her tiny hands and rests them on my cheeks. "I'm madly in love with you, Aiden. I have been for as long as I can remember. I'm sorry Miles was trying to make you jealous, it was stupid, and I hurt you. I'll never forgive myself for it. I need you to hear me when I say there is nothing going on with us. Miles is a good friend who thought he was helping. He didn't know that we had a break through. He just saw you behind us and acted on it." She leans in closer, her lips hovering close to mine. "I love you, Aiden Emerson. With everything in me, I love you. Please, forgive me," she pleads.

I lean in the rest of the way and gently press my lips to hers. I pull her into my lap and caress her face. I feel the wetness of her tears. I rest my forehead against hers. "I love you too, baby, so damn much it hurts." Then I crash my lips to hers, taking everything she's willing to give.

After we are both breathless, I slow the kiss and hug her tight. "So what does this mean, angel? Tell me what you want. Where do we go from here?" I fire question after question. My mind is racing, and so is my heart. I'm surprised I can even form a question, let alone get one past my lips.

"Well, I hope it means that we're together now. What I want is you, only you, and where do we go? Hopefully, we move forward together," she says, still resting her head against my chest. "What does this mean to you, Aiden? Tell me what you want. Where do you think we go from here?" She turns my questions around on me.

"This means you're mine. What I want is you, only you. Always you. Where do we go? Well, that's even easier. We move forward together and build a life together. You're it for me, angel. I'm irrevocably in love with you. You're stuck with me," I tease as I tickle her side.

She squirms until she is sitting up, straddling my lap. "I have very fond memories of us this way," she says with a wink.

"Really? I don't think I remember, you might have to demonstrate," I say, slipping my hands up under her shirt.

"Oh, I think that can be arranged," she says, melding her lips with mine.

# ~ 36 ~

## Hailey

Aiden's hands find my hips and he helps me find my rhythm. Our mouths are fused together, tongues dueling, and it's not enough. I want more of him. I want all of him. I break away from the kiss, my chest heaving with excitement. I slowly stand up. I can see the question in his eyes. I reach down, grab his hand, and pull him off the couch. I lead the way down the hall to my bedroom. Aiden stops me in front of his door.

"I need to see you in my bed. I've dreamed of that very thing for months. I'll just hold you if that's what you want, but I just need you with me…in my bed," he says, almost pleading.

I reach for the handle and push open the door. Aiden shuts it behind us and fastens the lock. Liam and Allison aren't here, but better safe than sorry. I walk to the bed and sit down. Aiden comes and stands between my legs. He rests his forehead against mine. "You are so beautiful. Are you really here? Please tell me this is not just a dream?" he asks me, my heart melting at his words.

"I'm here and I'm all yours."

His lips find mine. Aiden picks me up and moves me further onto the bed, never breaking our kiss. We are laying side by side and I still want more. I sit up and pull my sundress over my head. I can see the shock and appreciation in his eyes.

"Hailey, we don't have to-" I interrupt him with another kiss. I push his back down on the bed and I straddle his hips.

211

"Isn't this where we left off?" I ask.

He doesn't answer. Instead, his hands find my hips and he again helps me find my rhythm. I can tell that I'm close; that burning tightness is ready to consume me. Aiden sits up so we are chest to chest. He reaches around, unclasps my bra and throws it across the room. His lips instantly find a nipple while his hand teases and caresses the other. This is all it takes to throw me into full-blown orgasmic bliss. I throw my head back and scream out his name. "Aiden!"

This time is more intense and seems to last forever. When I finally come down to Earth, Aiden lays me down beside him and wraps his arms around me. I can feel his hardness through his khaki shorts pressing against my leg. I want to touch him. I want to give him what he just gave me. I want to make him fall apart at the seams.

I reach down, but hesitate. "Can I touch you?" I whisper, afraid that he's going to turn me down.

He engulfs my cheeks with his big strong hands. "Baby, you can do anything you want to me. I'm yours: heart, body, and soul."

I feel a rush of heat between my legs, holy shit, the affect those simple words have on me. Aiden lays on his back and I unbutton his shorts. I slowly slide the zipper down and gently stroke him through his boxer briefs. Aiden growls. I smile at the fact that it's me he wants, and it's me that's driving him crazy. Aiden lifts his legs to allow me to pull off his shorts. He takes it a step further, and slides off his boxer briefs and chucks them just like he did my bra. My eyes widen at the size of him, standing at attention for me. I take my hand and softly place my fingers around him. I can feel him pulsating in my hand. It's erotic and sexy, and I'm so turned on that I can barely focus.

Aiden gently brushes my hair out of my eyes. "I have no expectations for tonight. I would be fine just holding you all night long. You have to promise me that you'll stop when you reach your limit," he says with so much love in his eyes. *This is really happening!*

His words make me want to please him even more, to show him what this is for me. What he is for me. I begin to stroke him gently, and by Aiden's growls of pleasure, I'm doing a good job. I place kisses up his chest until I reach his neck. I nip and kiss him there, all the while, continuing to work him with my hand. Aiden runs his hands down my body until he finds the center of me. I feel him run his fingers through my folds, and the pleasure of his hands being there is like no other. This is all new to me, not just loving the man of my dreams, but all of it. I've been as far as kissing and groping under the shirt, but his lips are the only ones that have ever touched my body intimately. Only Aiden.

I bury my face in his neck, enjoying he sensation that his fingers are causing. "Can I go further, baby? Can I feel you from the inside?" he whispers.

"Please," I beg him.

He gently slides one of his fingers inside me, and the sensation has me begging for more. "You're so wet and tight. Has anyone else ever been here, baby?" he asks softy.

"No, Aiden. Please," I beg.

"Please what? Tell me what you need."

"More! I need more of you, all of you, now, please."

He increases his efforts by adding another finger and it feels amazing, but it's still not enough for me. I want him inside me, all of him.

I place my lips next to his ear. "Make love to me, please, Aiden."

His hand stills. "Hailey," he croaks, "I can't, not yet." I start to pull away at his rejection, but he grabs a hold and stops me. "Just listen, okay?" I nod my head. "Once I'm inside of you, you're mine. There will be no turning back. You need to take all the time you need to make sure that this is what you want, because when I make love to you, I won't ever be able to let you go. You are too fucking important to me, and I love you so damn much, without ever being inside of you. So when I finally am…yeah, you need to be sure."

"I don't need time, Aiden. I've loved you for a while now and I know you. I know how amazing you are, and I want nothing more than to be yours for as long as you'll have me."

"Forever," he says, capturing my lips with another scorching kiss until we are once again both breathless.

I pull back and look into his eyes. "Make love to me, baby," I say, and I can see that he isn't going to fight me.

"I don't have anything to protect you. I never planned on this, and I haven't been with anyone else in over a year…I'm sorry, we can't," he says, disappointment in his voice.

"Hold that thought." I jump out of bed and pull his t-shirt over my head. I rush to my room and dig through my bag. Luckily for him, I knew this is how I wanted things to go and I came prepared. I make a mad dash back to his room, shut the door, lock it, and rip his t-shirt from my body before crawling back in bed with him. I hand him the new unopened box of condoms and smile. "I wanted to be prepared if you were willing to take me back. This isn't a spur of the moment decision that I'm going to regret in the morning. This is our forever," I tell him.

Without another word, Aiden opens the box and pulls out a condom. He throws the rest of the box on the floor. He climbs between my legs and sits back on his. I watch in fascination as he opens the little silver packet and proceeds to sheath himself. "You have to promise me that if you need me to stop, you will tell me. You say stop and we're done. No pressure," he says softly as he rubs his erection through my folds.

"I won't say stop. I want you."

"I'll go slow. I don't want to hurt you."

I nod and he stills his erection at my entrance. He leans down and places a soft, tender kiss on my lips. "I love you, Hailey," he says as he slowly pushes inside.

There is a sharp burning and I tense at the pain. Aiden pauses, allowing me to adjust to his size and his entrance to my body. "Just breathe, baby," he tells me. After a few minutes, I relax under the onslaught of his tongue on my neck. Aiden notices. "All right, just a little more and I will be all the way in. I'll stop once I'm there and give you as much time as you need."

"Okay."

Aiden pushes in the rest of the way in one swift movement. He swallows my cries of pain with his kisses. "I'm so sorry, baby. Fuck, I hate that this hurts you."

I grab his face in my hands. "I want you to make love to me. I'm good. I promise. The pain is gone. Now, all I need is you."

Aiden studies me to make sure that I am indeed okay, before he rocks his hips into mine. Pleasure like I have never known consumes me. I wrap my legs around his waist and my arms around his neck and hold on.

"Baby, I'm sorry, but I'm close. You feel so amazing…can't…hold…on…much…longer," he pants.

"Aiden!" I scream as my orgasm tears through me.

"Hailey!" Aiden shouts. He slows his rhythm until he is completely spent.

I pull his chest to mine and hug him tight. "Thank you," I say into his ear. "I love you."

He pulls back resting his weight on his arms, careful not to crush me. "I love you. No going back, Hales. You're mine now."

# ~ 37 ~

# Aiden

*Holy. Fucking. Shit!* Never in my life have I felt anything like this. Being inside Hailey, making love to her, I have no words to describe this feeling, these emotions coursing through me. I hate to let go of her yet, but I need to get rid of the condom. I drop a kiss to her forehead. "I'll be right back, baby." I quickly jump out of bed and head to the bathroom. I dispose of the condom and wet a washcloth with warm water. I make my way back to the bed and sit on the edge. I tap her legs softy. "Open for me," I say. She does, no questions asked. I gently clean her up and toss the washcloth through the bathroom door. I'm not leaving her again, so that will have to do for now.

I crawl into bed next to her and pull her down on my chest. She fits perfectly. I pull the covers up over us and kiss her temple. "Sleep, baby. I love you."

"Love you," she says with a yawn.

I lay there holding her, gently stroking her back. I can't believe she's here. She's mine after all this time. I'm going to fight like hell, and tell her every day what she means to me. I want forever with this girl. I hug her tighter, close my eyes, and fall into the best night of sleep I can ever remember, holding my girl in my arms.

I wake the next morning to someone knocking on my bedroom door. Hailey grumbles, "go away" and scoots closer to me. I chuckle as I brush the hair from her face.

"Morning, angel."

The knocking continues. "Aiden, have you seen Hailey? She's not in her room." Allison asks through the door. Her voice is laced with concern.

Hailey giggles. "Aiden Emerson, you better not have a girl in there with you. Open this damn door," Allison seethes.

I smile at Hales. "I think you should get it. It's your giggling that pissed her off," I tease her.

"Ugh." Hailey climbs out of bed and throws me a pair of gym shorts. She grabs my shirt from the floor and slips it on over her head.

She starts for the door and I call out to her, "Hailey." She turns and I motion for her to come to me. She does. "No matter what, it's you and me. You're my girl, nothing is going to change that," I tell her.

She smiles her breathtaking smile, kisses my cheek, and saunters to the door shaking her fine ass as she goes. Damn minx.

She pulls open the door and Allison's mouth drops open. She takes Hailey in and what she's wearing. She looks over Hailey's shoulder and spots me sitting up in bed. Sans shirt. I smile and wave.

"Did you…are you…" Allison can't form a sentence, and I can't help but laugh at her.

Hailey looks over her shoulder and smiles at me. "Yeah, we did, and yeah, we are," she says, looking right at me. My hearts skips a beat just at the sight of her standing there in my shirt, voice still raspy with sleep. She fucking gorgeous and she's mine.

"Holy shit! Finally!" Allison screams as she tackles Hailey in a hug. I throw my head back and laugh.

Liam comes rushing into the room. "What's going on? Why are you yelling?" His eyes are roaming over Allison, making sure she's okay. After coming to the conclusion that she is, indeed, fine, his eyes move to Hailey. He takes in her appearance and I see the moment realization hits. "Are you happy, Hales?" he asks quietly.

"Deliriously," she replies.

A smile breaks across his face. "Finally, you two have come to your senses. Now maybe, I can have my best friend and my sister back," he teases.

I hop out of bed and join them at the door. I place an arm around Hailey's waist and haul her against my chest. "What's for breakfast?" I ask and we all laugh. Everything is right. Hales is mine and I couldn't be happier.

The rest of the week flies by. Hailey and Allison hang out while Liam and I are at camp. At night, I spend time with my girl, and make love to her. Tonight is her last night here. She has to go back tomorrow because she starts nursing school on Monday. It's going to kill me to let her go, but this is her dream. I want her to have everything she could ever want. I will be racking up some miles on the ol' Tahoe.

"So, long distance. You think we can do this?" she asks as we lay in bed.

"Yes. No question in my mind. You are my life, Hailey. This has been the best week of my existence, and I want nothing more than to tie you to my bed and keep you here, but I can't. You need to finish school and make your dreams come true. I'll be here when you're done. Actually, I'll be there to pack your ass up and move you here with me. One year, baby. Twelve months. We got this," I tell her.

"I'm going to miss you, miss sleeping in your arms," she says softly.

"I will be there as much as I can, and when you get a break from class, you come to me."

"We got this," she repeats my words.

I hold her tight, not looking forward to tomorrow. I close my eyes and drift off to sleep for the last night for a while with my girl in my arms.

# ~ five months later ~

# Aiden

The last few months have been sweet agonizing pleasure. It's been a little over five months since Hailey and I became an official couple, and I have never been happier in my life. It's hard going all week not seeing her, and away games sucked, but she traveled to a few that were close and she made every single home game. Hailey loves school, and that makes the separation a hell of a lot easier to take. It makes her happy, which makes me happy. I thought I loved her then, those feelings pale in comparison to how I feel about her now.

Today is the day that my best friend marries my sister. Liam and Allison are getting married. It's a small affair, just close friends and family. Allison doesn't have any family other than me and my parents, so they are keeping it simple. Hailey and I make up the entire wedding party as best man and maid-of-honor. She tried her dress on for me last night, and I just about swallowed my tongue. She takes my breath away every fucking time I look at her.

Liam, Allison, and our parents have been helping me with a surprise that I have planned for Hailey. Tonight, I'm going to ask her to marry me. I want every part of her engrained with every part of me, forever. I've been planning this for a while, since day one, I think. It was actually Allison who suggested I do it tonight. At first, I fought it, not wanting to take away from their day. They both insisted that it will just make the day more memorable. So here I am, in a small room in the reception hall. I'm standing on a ladder with glow-in-the-dark stars. I'm writing *Marry Me* on the ceiling. The inspiration comes from that night by the pond at Liam and Allison's engagement party. The stars were so bright that night, an amazing background to the start of our future. Even though that night ended badly, the start of it was spectacular and I remember every single fucking second of my time with her under the stars.

I place the final star as my cell rings. It's Liam.

"Hello?" I say climbing down the ladder. I could have paid someone to do this, but I wanted it to be me. It means more knowing that I did this for her.

"Where in the hell are you? Hailey is starting to freak that you're not here," he says, frustrated.

"Relax, man. I'm in the building. I was just finishing my surprise. My mom is going to take care of the champagne, and my dad has the ring for now. I have your ring for Allie in my pocket." I reach into my pocket for reassurance that it is, indeed, still there.

"Thank fuck!" Liam says. I hope I can hold it together a little better when Hales and I get our turn. Who am I kidding? I'll probably sob like a fucking baby at the relief that she is legally mine.

"I'm on my way," I tell him. I shut off the light and lock the door, placing the key in my pocket. I rush through a shower and dress quickly in my tux. My dad comes in to tell us that it's almost time. He also goads Liam, telling him how beautiful Allison looks. My dad is walking her down the aisle. I can still remember how nervous she was to ask him. My dad welled up with tears at her request. She is our family in every sense of the word.

The wedding is simple and elegant, and very much Allison. I can tell that she had a hand in every single detail of the day. She and Liam both are wearing permanent smiles. My hand slides into my pocket and I grasp the box that my father slipped me after my best man speech. It's time for me to surprise my girl and ask her to give me her forever. The song I requested begins to play. I chose Dierks Bentley "Breathe Me In". That's the same song that was playing at the engagement party when I asked her to take a walk with me. Fits well with the theme of the night.

Hailey is talking to our parents. They all know what's about to happen. My palms are sweaty. I know she loves me, but there is always the unknown fear of rejection. I walk up behind Hailey and place my hand on her hip. "Dance with me," I whisper in her ear. She looks over her shoulder at me, and smiles.

I grab her hand and lead her out to the dance floor. I pull her close and breathe her in, just like Dierks tells me to. Hailey goes up on her tiptoes and kisses me tenderly. This girl owns me. The song comes to an end and I almost miss it because of her kiss.

"Take a walk with me," I whisper. She smiles, the one that she reserves just for me, and I know she remembers. My plan is falling into place. I lead her to the hallway and pull a thin black scarf out of my pocket. "I have a surprise for you, baby," I tell her. "I need to place this over your eyes. I promise it won't be tight and I will not mess up your hair," I vow.

She laughs and there has never been a sweeter sound. "Who cares about my hair? The night is almost over," she says.

I gently place the blind fold over her eyes. I make sure it's not too tight. After I'm confident that she can no longer see, I place my hand in the small of her back and guide her down the hallway. I stop in front of the door. I reach into my pocket and pull out the key. I slide the key into the lock and it makes a clicking sound. "Aiden?"

"I just had to unlock the door, baby," I assure her, leading her into the room. I shut the door behind us and turn the lock back into place. I need this moment to just be ours, I can't risk our family busting in and ruining the moment.

I step behind Hailey and place a tender kiss at the base of her neck. The room is dark except for the glow of my heart spelled out in stars on the ceiling, *Marry Me*. Here goes nothing.

"Baby, can you tilt your head back for me and keep your eyes closed?"

"Yes," she whispers into the quiet room.

I feel my way to the blindfold and untie it. I slip it from her eyes and shove it into my pocket, replacing the ring box. I walk around to the front of her and go down on one knee.

"Open your eyes, angel," I say huskily.

I hear her gasp. "Aiden!" she says. I can hear the emotion in her voice. I clap my hands and a lamp turns on and illuminates the room with a soft glow. Yes, I used a clapper and I am proud of my well thought out eBay purchase.

I open the box; she places a hand over her mouth trying to drown out the sobs. She is crying big tears. If it weren't for the huge smile lighting up her eyes, I would be scared as hell, but the look in her face, she wants this and my confidence rises.

"Hailey, you are the love of my life, the most important person in my world. You never leave my mind no matter what's going on in my day. These past several months have been the happiest and the hardest of my life. I hate being away from you, but I love the fact that I know no matter where you are, you're mine and I'm yours. My love for you knows no bounds. I love you with every beat of my heart. Will you do me the incredible honor of being my wife?"

Hailey launches herself into my arms and we fall backwards. She kisses me hard. I laugh because I can only assume that this means she's saying yes, but I need to hear the words.

I sit up with her in my lap. I brush a loose tendril of hair from her eyes. I take the ring out of the box and slip it on her finger. "I need to hear you say it, baby."

"Yes! Yes! Yes! Aiden Emerson, you are my heart and I want nothing more than to be your wife.

I rest my forehead against hers. "Thank you for giving me your forever."

I hear cheers outside the door and realize our families must be out there eavesdropping. They had to have heard Hailey's triple yes. I laugh. "That would be our families," I tell her.

"Do they know?" she asks.

"Yes, they know. I had to ask your parents' for permission. I also discussed it with Liam, and by default, Allison. I told my parents because, well, they're my parents."

"You're a dream come true, Aiden Emerson."

"As are you, future Mrs. Emerson."

# contact Kaylee Ryan

**Facebook:** https://www.facebook.com/pages/Kaylee-Ryan-Author/589642871063467

**Goodreads:** http://www.goodreads.com/book/show/17838885-anywhere-with-you

**Twitter:** @author_k_ryan

**Website:** http://www.kayleeryan.com

## Other works by Kaylee Ryan

Anywhere With You – August 2013

# acknowledgements

I have so many people that I want to thank. First and foremost, my husband for your never ending support and encouragement. There is no way that I could have made it through this process without you. To my son for all the times that mommy needed just a few more minutes. I love you both!

To all of my new author friends, you ROCK! Your support means the world to me and I will be forever grateful. Our group discussions help me realize that we are all out there doing what we love and supporting one another is essential to each of us and our success. (AS101)

Sarah Hanson of Okay Creations, another amazing cover. Thank you so much for your amazing talent!

Mary from Mary Elizabeth's Crazy Book Obsession, girl you are amazing! Organizing the cover reveal, release day blitz, to the blog tour and creating the trailer. Your support means the world to me and I could not have done this without you!

Tiffany Aleman and Ashley Poch thank you for allowing an excerpt of More With You to be included in your new release Serenity Falls.

Tiffany Aleman thanks for the talks and support. I am truly blessed that we are friends and I can only hope that I am able to provide you with the same support that you have given me. I love ya girl!

To all of the bloggers out there...Thank you so much. Your never ending support of the indie community is greatly appreciated. I know that you don't hear it enough so hear me now. I appreciate each and every one of you and the support that you have given me. Love Between the Sheets, Just Booked, Helenas Book Obesession, Bad and Dirty Books, LipSmackin Good Books, Stephanie's Book Reports, Best Sellers & Best Stellars of Romance, Jodie's Wine List. Thank you to all of you for the support that you have given me. I know that there are many others who have supported me through this process and I thank each and every one of you from the bottom of my heart.

To Tami of Integrity Formatting you make it all come together in a pretty little package. Thank you!

To my street team, you ladies know who you are. I will never be able to tell you how much your support means. I will never forget all that you have done for me. Thank you!

Last but not least, to the readers. Without you none of this would even be worth the effort. I truly love writing and I am honored that I am able to share that with you. Thank you to each and every one of you for reading **More With You**.

39111722R00139

Made in the USA
Middletown, DE
05 January 2017